DARK
TAAL

Book one of the Foundation Stone series

Dean G E Matthews

This book is published by
Grosvenor House Publishing Ltd
Link House
140 The Broadway, Tolworth, Surrey, KT6 7HT.
www.grosvenorhousepublishing.co.uk

This book is a work of fiction. Any resemblance to
people or events, past or present, is purely coincidental.

A CIP record for this book
is available from the British Library

ISBN 978-1-83975-608-5

CONTENTS

Acknowledgements

To Maryanne,
for putting up with me, my computer tantrums and
being instrumental in completing this book.

And to my mother for her unending support.

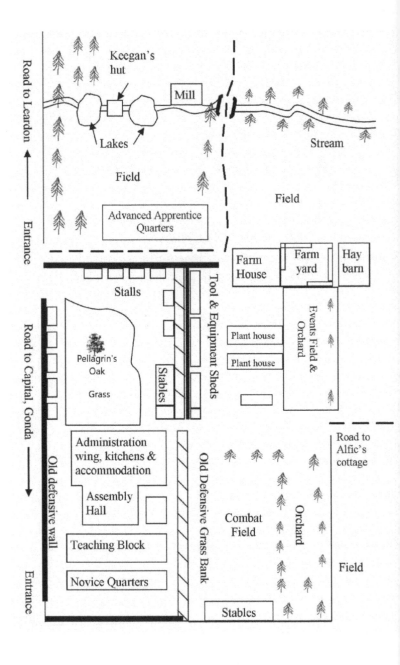

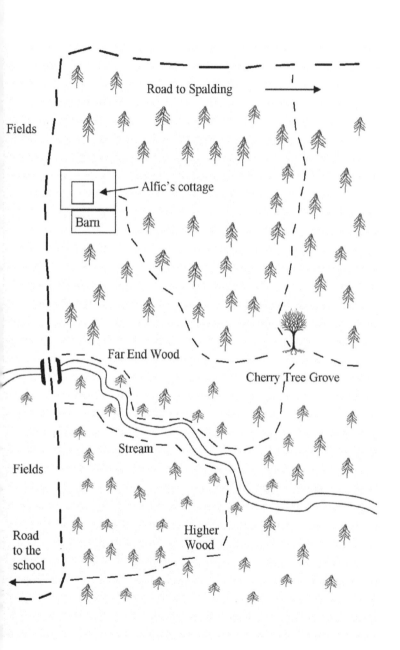

INTRODUCTION

The Dark Taal is about Aridain Bruin, a young boy whose destiny it is to find and destroy the fabled Firebrand and Chimera stones. He was born into the world of Aymara, currently a world blighted by suspicion and uncertainty.

Thousands of years ago, the gods, in order to bring balance and harmony, made the Firebrand stone and the Chimera stone. The Firebrand stone was born of darkness and the Chimera stone born of light. The gods made them accessible to the many races of Aymara, and their balancing influence worked for a time. However, as the races advanced and reason prevailed, the Chimera stone was forgotten over time and disappeared; leaving the Firebrand stone's evil unchecked and the world is once more ravaged by unremitting war. That was, until a Mage, by the name of Pellagrin, and his followers stole the Firebrand stone from his evil brother, Chador. He split it into four and then hid the segments from the gaze of the power hungry.

Peace reigned for a time, but as war threatens the land of Durbah and the surrounding lands once more, the gods decide to act and Aridain is born, championed by the goddess Seline. His magic, uncontrolled and unrestrained, attracts a dark opposite, championed by the dark god Fornax; this creature is destined to kill Aridain, salvage the stones and usher forth a new reign of terror;

but they are not alone. Also seeking the stones is Aridain's evil uncle, a dark wizard called Kuelack, who also seeks dominion over the six kingdoms and the world of Aymara.

With his dark opposite stalking him, Aridain, with the aid of friends and family, must quickly learn who he is and control the magic that will aid him in his quest to defeat the Dark Taal and then find and destroy the stones.

Prologue

The howling wind shrieked like tormented banshees, bending and buckling the ornate planting and shrubbery that surrounded the imposing manor house. Dwarfing the meagre timber and straw dwellings that surrounded it, the manor house's stone-built walls and hardwood windows stood steadfast against the storm's onslaught as, gathered around a luxuriously swathed four-poster bed in nervous expectation, a family sheltered within one of its sumptuously furnished candlelit bedrooms.

'How much longer, Mother?'

'Stop pacing and be patient, Alfic.'

'If you say "be patient" one more time Vara, I swear I'll throw my husband at you.'

'It's no good getting cross with me, Lascana. We cannot rush these things. Your son will arrive when he is good and ready.'

'I just hope that this obstinacy isn't a sign of things to come, Vara,' gasped Lascana irritably. Then, relenting, she asked, 'Do you have any more of your painkilling concoction? I feel like I'm about to give birth to a horse.'

Joining his father by the window, Alfic peered out into the rain-lashed night as yet another bolt of lightning split the darkness with an accusing finger. 'That strike was close, Father. What a night! I'm glad we're tucked away indoors.'

'It's as if Mother Nature herself is objecting to this birth,' said Perak, peering outside and then glancing hesitantly at his son; suddenly he stumbled backwards with a yelp of surprise as a large bird, illuminated by another intense flash, appeared outside the window where it hovered for an instant before disappearing from view.

Alfic bent down to help his father up off the floor and inquired, 'Are you alright?'

'I'm fine,' he said, straightening out his tunic and returning to the window. 'Birds are normally tucked away on a night like this.'

'Probably lost in the storm and, seeing the light, it sought shelter,' replied Alfic matter-of-factly.

'You think? Look there.'

'What is it now?' despaired Vara in a tone that implied now wasn't the right time. 'Can't you see we're busy here?'

'The creatures of the woodland,' he exclaimed, cupping his chunky hands against the rain-streaked glass and peering into the gloom, 'They're gathering in the garden.'

'You're seeing things, you old fool,' said Vara irritably.

'If you don't believe me... take a look!'

Joining Perak, Alfic peered through the glass into the rain-lashed night.

'Father's right; there are all manner of creatures out there.'

Turning towards his son, Perak hissed, 'Why would such a myriad of creatures gather together outside in our garden, and in this weather?'

'Any ideas, Mother?' inquired Alfic.

'No, I don't, now stop wasting my time, the pair of you.'

'I don't care if the Blood God, Fornax, himself is here. Just deliver this baby,' barked Lascana. 'This is taking far too lo…'

'Lascana?' cried Alfic anxiously, rushing over to her side. 'Well, I'll be…'

'Vara, look! The spirits of the woods are here in our house,' said Perak reverently, as pixies, sprites and dapperlings (small furtive half pixie, half moth like creatures) appeared together with a myriad of fairy folk, fluttering and skipping on gossamer wings and quicksilver feet into the bedroom, gathering at the foot of the bed.

Bathed in the glow of fire imps and with the pain of her labours all but forgotten; Lascana stared in wonder at the bizarre gathering.

'What are they doing here?' she asked as Alfic moved protectively to her side, his hands raised to shoo them away.

'Alfic, no! This is a blessing to be sure,' declared Perak.

'Says you,' said Alfic, standing uneasily as a cluster of sprites, clad in moss and lichen and their skin shimmering with multi-coloured light, flew tentatively towards Lascana.

'What are they doing?' asked Vara, watching the sprites warily.

'Be quiet for once in your life and watch, Vara,' hissed Perak. 'This is a special moment. Fairy folk never leave the protection of the woods without good reason.'

Carrying a small plant bundle between them, six sprites laid the small garland on Lascana's pregnant body and then, inclining their tiny heads as if in homage, returned to the end of the bed where they settled down to watch, gathering excitedly with their brethren.

'What's this?' asked Alfic sceptically, reaching for the bundle.

'Alfic, the pain has eased,' smiled Lascana, squeezing her husband's hand. She looked gratefully towards the sprites. 'I don't know what you did or what you're doing here, but thank you,' she said with a smile.

'Does anybody else think this is all a little bizarre?' asked Alfic.

'More than a little,' agreed Vara.

Suddenly they all jumped at another crack of thunder as the candles flickered and spluttered in a sudden gust of wind that gushed up the stairs, causing the bedroom door to slam shut and the shadows to dance.

'That was too close. Another one like that and I won't need to push,' said Lascana.

Squeezing his wife's hand reassuringly and parting her fine auburn hair which, normally so perfect, was now plastered to the sides of her face, Alfic said gently, 'It's only lightning.'

Then kissing her forehead tenderly, he said grimly, 'When we're about to give birth, the last thing we need is the help of woodland sprites; chaos and uncertainty accompany them whenever they appear.'

Pulling violently on Alfic's arm and staring threateningly into his eyes, Lascana barked, 'We're about to give birth! I don't see you lying exhausted on the bed; I've been at this for the last six hours.'

'You know what I mean. Are you alright?'

Relenting, she said, 'I will be when our son makes an appearance.'

'Any explanations, Mother, as to what's going on?' asked Alfic, running a hand through his thick black hair.

'Why do you keep asking me?' said Vara, walking to the end of the bed, scattering the fairy folk.

'The occult is your forte,' replied Alfic.

'We, that is I, deal in the here and now, not hearsay and speculation. Now no more talk, it's time to push, Dear; your son is about to make an appearance,' Vara announced, her red-rinsed hair akin to a bloated red sun rising above stark white mountain peaks as she peered above the sheets at Lascana. A much louder crack of thunder accompanied her statement.

'I'll just wait outside in the hall,' smiled Perak, sheepishly tucking his shirt into his breeches. 'This waiting, this storm, it's all really getting on my nerves,' he declared.

'You do that,' mumbled Vara impassively.

'Vara, it's alright,' gasped Lascana.

As Lascana pushed, the rain relented, the wind died and an eerie silence settled over the house; the only sounds were Lascana's laboured exertions. With one final effort a baby's cry filled the silence, accompanied by one last tremendous crack of thunder that made them all jump in fright as Vara, with a look of triumph, stood at the end of the bed holding Alfic and Lascana's son wrapped in a towel.

The door burst open suddenly, and Perak exploded into the room. 'I heard the baby's cry. Well done, Lascana! A good night's work, I'd say.'

'She hasn't been digging over the veg border, you old fool,' said Vara tersely, handing Lascana the infant and then walking over to the window. 'You men really have no idea, do you?'

'Father, I want you to say hello to Aridain Bruin, my son,' announced Alfic, proudly gesturing to the softly cooing bundle wrapped in Lascana's arms.

'Welcome to the world, Aridain Bruin,' beamed Perak, bowing gracefully.

Alfic joined Vara at the window and, after peering up into the rapidly clearing sky and the now tranquil garden, said, 'The animals, the storm, they are all gone as if they were never here.' Studying her face intently, Alfic asked, 'Mother, what are you thinking?'

'Nothing, it's nothing.'

She then turned and walked purposefully toward Lascana. 'Now give your son to me, so I can bathe him.' She gently took Aridain from Lascana's arms then with a flourish, and shadowed by the fairy folk chattering and chirping excitedly, turned and headed down the dark, spacious, ornament-filled hallway, her ankle-length gold and green gown billowing sail-like behind her.

'Vara, wait!'

'What is it, Perak?'

'You may have them fooled, but you can't fool me,' he hissed, spinning her around by the elbow and staring at her intently with narrowed chocolate brown eyes and a suspicious look. 'I've known you too long.'

'I have no idea what you're talking about.'

'The animals watching in the garden, these fairy folk,' he said, indicating the creatures following attentively, 'and the storm that suddenly dissipated with that final clap of thunder. What is it that you're not telling us, what just happened?'

'All just coincidence,' she smiled.

'Coincidence! During a storm in the middle of the night, magical creatures don't just leave their home and gather in and around people's houses for no reason.'

Vara sighed. 'As Aridain grew inside Lascana, I recognised the child had power, but this bizarre series of events… I can't, I won't speculate until I'm certain.'

'But…'

'But nothing; right now, I have things to do, so go and make yourself useful, relight the candles.'

'Don't think this is the end of it, Vara Bruin,' warned Perak.

Entering the washroom, she placed a candle on the tabletop and with a snap of her fingers; it burst into flame. Waving annoyingly at the imps and sprites that gathered around, she poured a jug full of warm water into a bowl and then slowly washed her grandson; his pale skin glowing softly in the candlelight. Then wrapping him as he became agitated, she set him down among silky soft cushions on the tabletop and kissed his forehead, 'Sshhh, don't fret, little one, you won't come to any harm, I swear.'

She shook her head in consternation. Perak was right; the storm, the creatures, these events were too much of a coincidence; this was not how things were supposed to be. Then, without warning, the candles spluttered and died in an icy gust of wind, and the room was suddenly bathed in an ephemeral white light. Sensing an unfamiliar presence, Vara quickly gathered the infant in her arms and watched, fascinated, as the fairy folk gathered around a saintly figure that had appeared in the doorway.

'You will have to do more than swear, Vara Bruin.'

Dressed in shimmering elegant white robes, the apparition's indomitable but kind bearing immediately caused her to feel at ease. 'Do not be alarmed, I wish no harm to you, the boy or his family.'

'Who are you spirit, what do you want?' asked Vara.

'I am here to honour the Elemental, "The One" destined to destroy the stones and restore balance.'

'The next Male Balefire?' declared Vara in disbelief.

'Why do you refuse to believe what you know to be true, Vara Bruin?' said the apparition, gliding forward slowly. 'You know of what I speak.'

'But how can that be? Legend says that the Firebrand stone is destroyed and the Chimera stone probably so, they are gone from the world…'

'There is every need, Vara Bruin. I failed in my attempt to destroy the Firebrand stone and only succeeded in splitting it into four segments. I hid them and propagated the lie that I destroyed it. Now the burden is greater than it has ever been. The gods have decreed that Aridain is tasked not only to destroy the Firebrand stone but the Chimera stone as well; before the Dark Creature can procure them.'

'How can this be? Only one of his parents has magic, and his ability is limited.'

'You have felt the child's power. He is akin to a brightly burning star. His magic and his life force will grow to be brief but powerful, tuned to one task only.'

'But how…'

'He must find a way.' The apparition tilted its head. 'Why so bitter, Vara Bruin? It is a great honour.'

'I have read the ancient chronicles; it is an "honour" I would wish on no one, especially my own grandson.'

'Do not fret, Vara Bruin; with our protection he has more than an even chance.'

Vara stared intently at the apparition with clear, grey eyes. She then scrutinised the sprites flitting around the apparition, attentive and unafraid. 'Who are you to make such a promise, and what do you mean, "with our protection"?'

'Search your feelings, and the answer will become clear.'

She looked at the floor, her eyes searching in the deafening silence. 'Your attire is that of the Dragon Lords of the northern lands. Pellagrin... you're Dragon Lord Pellagrin, the founder of the school and our civilization!'

'Very astute, Vara Bruin.'

Pellagrin's apparition slowly extended its hand, placing it over the child's head. After mumbling a few words, it then disappeared.

'Wait! Come back, what must I do? How do I protect him?' Vara cried. Then, making up her mind on a course of action, she hurried from the room with the infant Aridain in her arms.

As the storm raged and at the exact time of Aridain's birth, a pinprick of intense darkness formed, born of violence and dark elemental magic. The pinprick then ignited with the same powerful bolt of lightning, followed by a deafening crack of thunder that reverberated throughout the night. The darkness grew and expanded like a living thing; liquid yet solid. Then, with an ear-deafening implosion, the darkness drew the clouds, the trees, and even the night itself toward it like a magnet. In the silence, a small shadow-less creature resembling a piece of black obsidian in the form of a new-born lay prone in the leaf litter. The creature, looking like a shard of night, that if looked upon would not appear wholly normal, stared blissfully upwards into the clear sky with citrine yellow eyes and wailed into the night. The grief-stricken sound causing the people and animals that heard it to flee in dread and cower in their homes. Searching the blackness with its small nose twitching, the creature stared eagerly at the entrance to a nearby labyrinth of holes set into a hillock. The creature bared rows of small sharp incisor teeth and then crawled with spindly appendages across the damp forest floor. Its insatiable hunger awoken; it was drawn towards the warmth radiating from the creatures within the bank.

CHAPTER ONE

TORSK

The virion cat crept silently through the night on thick, padded paws, its dense black and iron grey-streaked fur ruffled by gusting chilly winds; its long, tufted ears and dark eyes alert for the slightest sight or sound. Ignoring a tasty field mouse that scavenged for a meal amongst the undergrowth, just beyond its reach, the cat stared upwards instead, following a barn owl, which flew silently overhead on gossamer wings; the cat's eyes narrowing as the owl screeched into the silence. Content that it wasn't being followed, the cat licked at its soft fur then continued on its way cautiously, silently, through the trees and wilting foliage of the undergrowth which was covered with late winter snows, towards a large stable block.

Unnerved, chargers, mules and shire horses plus two vicious-looking killdeers, (carnivorous deer with sharp antlers, claws and teeth), poked their heads out of the stable doors one by one, their restive breathing clearly visible in the frosty winter air. Keeping to the shadows, the cat, its ears flattened, sat on its haunches and stared out across the expansive field beyond, then at a line of majestic chestnut trees silhouetted dark against the veil of stars.

Closing its eyes, the virion cat bowed its head as if in respect, its form changing and growing until instead of a lithe, efficient killing machine there stood an elderly, naked, grey-haired man. Sprightly for his age, he stepped gingerly over to the stables and searching around the back; he retrieved a bundle of garments he'd hidden there earlier. Setting his jaw, he dressed hastily in the chilly night air and then calmed the startled creatures housed inside with a smile and a gentle touch. His thoughts then turned to the events that had led to this illicit meeting in the middle of the night. It was a meeting sparked by his fear for the lives of students and teachers alike. It was a meeting that, if discovered by the Sivan council, would result in his banishment, or worse; but the risk was worth it. What he had uncovered was spreading through the school like a malignant cancer. However, knowledge of a conspiracy was nothing without proof. Until he was certain he couldn't approach the one man he could trust with his knowledge, the Head of the Sivan council, Almagest. He was the only person with power enough to stand against Kuelack. Third on the Sivan council, Kuelack was a man who craved power, demanded obedience and desired submission. Two nights ago, one of his students had approached him, claiming he had vital information and to meet him here at midnight. It was an opportunity to expose Kuelack's schemes; it was an opportunity he could not pass up.

A sound to his right caused him to turn, but before he could issue a challenge, his arms were forcibly clamped against his sides by invisible fingers of power that held him tight. A slight, hooded figure emerged from the shadows dressed in grey, utilitarian clothing and a cape.

'Torsk, is that you?' hissed a female voice. 'What are you doing here?'

Grunting in pain, he said, 'Mistress Cardia, I might ask you the same question.' Looking down at his clamped arms, then back at her, he said, 'Do you mind?'

'Not until you tell me what you're doing here.'

'I am here to meet… a student,' he growled.

'A student?' she inquired, pulling back her hood to reveal a thick head of dark hair and staring at him guardedly with dark, surprised eyes.

'Release me and I'll tell you.'

Suddenly, free of his invisible bonds, Torsk dropped to the floor. Somewhat annoyed and brushing at his velvet robe, Torsk continued, 'I've been investigating a conspiracy at this school, and I'm here because one of my students said he had information regarding the said conspiracy. By your reaction it seems so are you.'

'Correct. On Almagest's authority, I'm investigating certain allegations. This student is not a person to be trusted, so when I saw you, I feared it was a trap.'

'I think it still is.' Torsk smiled in the dark, knowing he may have gained an ally. 'It's such a relief to know I'm not alone in this, I didn't know who to trust or who to talk…'

Suddenly they were hurled through the air by powerful hammer blows of force. Sprawled upon the floor of the stable yard holding his stomach and gasping for air, Torsk peered across at Cardia, who lay at the base of a tree trunk and who, like him, was struggling to gain her feet. Coughing and gasping for air, he looked up at the sound of hooves to see the dark, sleek shape of a killdeer charging with its head stooped. Realising the danger, Torsk climbed to his feet as a second killdeer appeared from out of the gloom. Too slow, he felt sharp antlers and claws rip into his body as it tossed him into the air and then trampled him underfoot. Lying prostrate on the stable yard floor, his body twisted and broken, Torsk searched the night with darkening vision. The killdeer had disappeared as if they had been part of some agonising nightmare and in the silence across the stable yard the joint head of the school stared back with unseeing eyes. Then, another crunching impact lifted him from the ground. Spiralling through the air he came to an abrupt jolt as he impacted with something solid. As darkness took him, he stared upwards from the base of a large tree trunk. Before his eyes dimmed, it dawned on him that from the moment he had accepted this invitation; he was destined to die.

CHAPTER TWO

THE END OF INNOCENCE

Sat sullenly in his utilitarian horse and trap, Perak Bruin urged his gelding, Midge, through the village of Spalding. It had been his home now for the past forty years. He watched as people scurried busily to and from the brightly garnished shops that encircled the village square. Market stalls were erected beneath the magnificent copper-leaved beech tree at its centre, which had grown there since before even the village elders could remember. Spalding was a village where everything and anything was sold, from ordinary day-to-day objects to the exotic and the bizarre. The wheelwright Spalding's, together with its ancillary companies of wagon makers and blacksmiths, was the largest employer in the area. An ancient house of worship, dedicated to the earth goddess, Seline, had been built nearby, together with The Corner House Tavern; both were popular stopovers, visited by people from all over the realm on their way to the school and the capital, Gonda.

Turning to Vara in an attempt to break the stony silence, Perak asked, 'Are you warm enough?'

Her stern, angular features cast in an unsympathetic expression, Vara replied curtly, 'I'm fine.'

Urging Midge into a trot, Perak hurried past the local house of worship and cursed when several of the ever-vigilant travelling vendors, eager to sell their wares, surrounded the trap, one selling locally sourced truffles, another selling rare spices he claimed were from the Broken Lands far to the south, while another offered so-called magical artefacts from the volcanic land of Zapata to the north.

'No, no and no,' shouted Perak, refusing their enthusiastic advances. He then urged Midge down Spalding's main street. 'Can't you curse them or something, Vara?' he said irritably.

With the street traders struggling to keep up, he headed purposefully out of the village along the cobbled road leading past his home, a house that, according to Vara, should convey to the populace an impression of what could be achieved if you had ambition and the money to back that ambition. Proud of his accomplishment, it was the first three-storey house in the village to have a tiled roof, positioned so that anyone travelling up the road would gain an impressive view of it. Once complete, he had turned to Vara stating categorically, "I have built the home you wanted, now the only way I'll leave this house is feet first."

Coming from a poor background, Perak just felt privileged to have saved enough money to afford and live in such a grand house. Over a period of time, their children had left one by one to seek their own way in the world. To Perak's disappointment their youngest son,

Kuelack, and to a certain extent their daughter, Magen, continued to be dissatisfied with life despite his best efforts. They were living proof of what he already knew, that no matter how much wealth a person obtains in life, it never guarantees their happiness or satisfaction, leaving them always craving more.

Of all of their children, only Alfic was really happy, sharing his own appreciation of the world around him and living a simple life without self-indulgence. At least his grandson, Aridain, would grow up living in the countryside, under Alfic's care, appreciating the true beauty and riches of this world. In contrast, he feared Magen's children would grow up spoilt and in ignorance of the world's true riches.

Waving to Hennas, the blacksmith, and the village thatcher, Jesra, sat precariously repairing Hennas' roof, Perak urged Midge past blossoming orchards and recently planted fields as the village gave way to the countryside. Rival male skylarks trilled raucously overhead, and a pair of brimstone butterflies danced and frolicked along a hedgerow, enticed out into the open by the warm early spring sunshine. They trundled across Spalding Common, an expansive area dotted here and there with large ash and oak trees, passing villagers grazing sheep, goats and cattle. Then they descended into a deep-cut ravine where large hawthorn trees ablaze with white and pink flowers dominated. Crossing the stream, they followed the track across a marshy field festooned with pink and white snake's head flowers and wild hyacinths bobbing in the breeze, the fresh fragrant scent causing Perak to inhale exuberantly.

'Doesn't that smell make you feel great to be alive, Vara?'

'Sweet-smelling flowers do not constitute happiness, Perak Bruin.'

Ignoring her moodiness and whistling a cheery tune, Perak steered Midge along the path that levelled out beside the stream. They continued to trot for another mile, crossing the brook again, disappearing beneath the enchanted oak canopy of Farend Wood. Primroses abounded on the woodland floor and Perak, in a vain attempt to engage Vara, brought to her attention the fresh greenery of numerous spring plants that were beginning to push through the dense undergrowth.

Turning from the splendour of the sun-dappled track in an effort to break the uncomfortable silence, he said, 'So, Aridain tells me you've been intensifying his teaching recently.'

'Did he now?'

'He's complaining it's taking away his adventuring time,' smiled Perak.

'It's nothing he can't handle.'

'Any particular reason?' inquired Perak, looking at her with the piercing gaze of an inquisitor.

'It's simple; school is just around the corner. There's nothing wrong with being prepared.'

'Even though witchcraft isn't my cup of tea, I understand it's in our grandson's best interest to learn all he can before he enrols at Pellagrin's, but don't take me for a fool, Vara. According to Aridain, you're teaching him some pretty advanced stuff; care to share?' he smiled sardonically.

Vara looked at him questioningly. 'No need to feel threatened, Perak. Aridain will always enjoy your woodland walks far more than my ethics and doctrine,' she snapped. 'As you say, it's in his nature.'

Scanning the dense canopy, then the surrounding woodland, Perak said, 'Yes, thankfully he's not the power-hungry kind…'

'What's the matter, Perak?'

'Something's not right.'

'You're imagining things.'

Abruptly the pleasantness of the ride changed, and the woodlands became quiet; Midge snorted nervously.

'What is it, boy?' Grasping the reins firmly, Perak brought the trap to a stop. Suddenly they heard the echo of cracking branches accompanied by high-pitched screeching, yelping, and harsh fear-filled snorting.

'Animals and creatures of the woods are coming closer; it sounds like they're terrified.'

'Then keep going; we don't want to be in the way.'

Suddenly, a red deer stag burst through the trees and bounded towards them, followed by more deer and all manner of beasts fleeing through the undergrowth.

Over the fear-filled wailing and snorting, Perak shouted, 'Something's really spooked them.'

'Go faster!' shouted Vara.

Urging Midge onwards, Perak insisted, 'I'm trying'.

Perak's desperate urging was too little, too late; led by the magnificent antler-crowned stag, the deer herd charged toward the trap.

'Vara, follow my lead and hold on tight,' shouted Perak who, in an attempt to counter the crazed beasts' attack, steered the trap sideways. There was a horrific rattling thud as the trap veered under the stag's initial impact. As more of the herd collided with the trap, it toppled on to its side, throwing Vara and Perak from the carriage into the undergrowth amidst pounding hooves. Despite this, Perak kept a tight hold of the reins. As Midge, the terrified stallion, leapt and pranced in an attempt to join the many woodland animals in flight, he dragged Perak, together with the trap, through the undergrowth and across the woodland floor.

Gaining his feet, Perak pulled Midge to a stop and scanned the woods, relieved to find that the impromptu stampede had ended as quickly as it had started. 'It's all right, Midge, they're gone; it's over.' He then looked back to see Vara climbing to her feet. 'Are you alright?'

'I'll be fine,' Vara snapped, brushing herself down.

Perak then looked around at the sounds of irate grunting and squealing as, crazed with fear, a family of enraged warthogs charged towards them.

'Vara, run, shelter behind the trap.'

'Run? I don't run!' screamed Vara.

'You have to hurry, run, now!'

Even as he warned her, Perak knew Vara wouldn't make it and, fearing for her life, he ran and rugby-tackled her to the floor. Shielding his wife, Perak wrapped his arms about her protectively and gritted his teeth, steeling himself against the inevitable. He felt Vara struggle beneath him as all around the warthogs attempted to sink their teeth into anything within striking distance. He felt the searing pain of sharp teeth and gouging tusks as they lay prone among pigs' trotters and their enraged squealing.

'Release me!' shouted Vara, who was now struggling violently. 'Release me now.'

'Temper, temper!' he mocked. 'I know you're uncomfortable with intimacy, but is that all the thanks I get for saving your life?'

'Any excuse with you, isn't it?'

'And with you it's any excuse not to,' he said sadly.

'Is it still here?' said Vara dispassionately, dusting herself down.

'Is what still here?' snapped Perak.

'Whatever spooked the wildlife,' Vara muttered irately.

'How would I know?' he said, peering anxiously into the trees.

Approaching Midge calmly, he whispered, 'At least you appreciate me, eh?' Then, turning to Vara, he insisted, 'Come on, help me right the trap. Grab the end of the reins and tie them to the rail!'

With the ends tied, Perak urged Midge gently forward, and slowly the gig toppled back on to its wheels.

Then, with Midge hooked up once more, Vara climbed back into the trap. 'No more dramas,' she said, looking nervously about. 'Let's get out of these woods before we encounter any more disgruntled wildlife intent on killing us.'

As they topped the rise, Alfic's cottage came into view, the sight dispelling Perak's anxiety. 'Well, this is one journey we won't forget in a hurry,' he said, indicating his torn and ripped clothing while rubbing at his cuts and bruises. 'I wonder what could have spooked the woodland creatures like that?'

'I don't know and right now I don't care,' said Vara irritably. 'Let's just get to the cottage, shall we?'

'Aridain! Come away from those animals at once,' called Lascana, shaking her head in consternation. She dropped her washing basket and rushed out of the front gate, followed by Chipper, their chocolate Doberman.

Hurrying across the road, she reached over the wooden fence that separated the field from the lane and held out her hands.

'Aridain,' she scolded, 'Come here right now!'

Aridain, who was sitting quietly among a herd of long-horned oxen, turned at his mother's insistent calls.

'But, Mummy, they won't hurt me, honest; they tell me so all the time.'

'Yes, Darling, so you say, but they are still very large animals and might hurt you by accident. Now do as you're told and come here to me, now,' ordered Lascana.

Stroking one of the cattle tenderly, Aridain said, 'Bye-bye Daisy, see you tomorrow.' Then, skipping across the field, he jumped into Lascana's arms.

'How many times do I have to tell you, Aridain Bruin? You have to be more careful; the world can be a dangerous place.'

Aridain looked up at her with innocent eyes, kissed her on the cheek, and then wriggled from her arms. 'I told you, I'm always careful, Mummy; you don't have to worry about me.'

Shaking her head despairingly, she closed the front gate and looked up at the cotton-wool-like clouds racing across the early morning spring sky, then at their modest cottage with smoke rising from its lime-washed chimney. Formerly an old army sentry post, Alfic had transformed it from a stark, utilitarian building into a warm, comfortable home.

Humming contentedly, she hung out the rest of the clothing and carried the washing basket inside. Then, picking up the slops bucket from the kitchen, she carried it down the stone path to the pigsty and hen houses located at the bottom of the garden beneath the trees. As she approached, the chickens ran eagerly towards her, followed closely by the pigs, squealing hungrily.

'Yes, all right, patience, patience, you'll all get your fair share,' she chuckled.

On her return, Lascana made her way to the small wooden barn beside the cottage, selected some vegetables from a large wooden stand and carried them to the kitchen. Returning to the barn, to gather some logs stacked just inside the main doors that faced the lane, she jumped back in alarm and let out a shriek as something large and furry scurried from beneath the pile.

'Huron's beard,' she exclaimed. *Cursed timber rats are eating the stores again,* she thought. *Alfic assured me he'd dealt with them.*

'Mummy, it's Uncle Keegan,' screamed Aridain, suddenly bounding into the barn with Chipper prancing and cavorting excitedly beside him.

'So, how many rats have you discovered this time?' chuckled Keegan, poking his head around the door.

'Oh, I'm fine, by the way,' she replied sarcastically.

Keegan wasn't actually Aridain's uncle, but an old friend of Alfic's. He had thick black sideburns that were tinged with grey that framed his jovial weathered face, and he had a gold front tooth that had been fitted after losing the original. Dressed in a simple green and brown jacket and fur-lined leggings, his long, unkempt hair sprouted like a mop from beneath a weathered trilby hat, which was topped off with a large pheasant's feather; he looked like an archetypal gamekeeper.

'Don't worry, Mum, me and Chipper will catch the rat.'

Suddenly there was a flurry of activity and the loyal canine, closely followed by Aridain, ran from the barn, shaking the furry offender between his teeth and causing Keegan to dodge sideways.

'Chipper, watch where you're going. You nearly knocked Uncle Keegan over,' scolded Aridain, shaking his finger sternly.

Chipper dropped the limp rat at their feet and then, with his tongue hanging out and his tail wagging, looked up with large innocent eyes.

'Your dog definitely has a loathing for timber rats,' smiled Keegan, ironically, stroking the Doberman affectionately. He then held up the dead rat for Lascana to see.

Bolting for the cottage and eyeing the carcass fearfully, Lascana shouted, 'Not funny.'

'Mummy doesn't like timber rats,' said Aridain, seriously.

'Yes, thank you, young man,' said Lascana tersely, watching from the kitchen door.

'Don't worry, Aridain, I'll save your mother from the dead, ferocious rat,' announced Keegan heroically, who, with hands on hips, puffed out his chest.

Despite her annoyance, Lascana couldn't help but smile when the gamekeeper was around; his cheery demeanour always seemed to lighten the mood.

'I can see why you live on your own. No woman would put up with you.'

Keegan, bowing regally, winked at Aridain. 'Lascana, you know you are the only woman for me.'

'You're funny, Uncle Keegan,' giggled Aridain.

'That's one way of describing him,' said Lascana sceptically.

Keegan then took his rucksack stuffed with poisons, snares, and traps from his shoulder and rummaged through the contents.

'Aridain,' he said, 'I have something for you.'

'I know, it's a pen set for when I go to school. My mum bought it for you to give to me.'

'That's right, so that you can…. write all that… knowledge… is that right, Lascana?'

'Young man, have you been peeking at your presents again?' despaired Lascana.

'No, Mum, I heard Keegan say so.'

'When?' asked Keegan, perplexed, studying Aridain's expectant face.

'Just now; you also said that I'll be much happier when I see the shield you bought to match my sword,' beamed Aridain.

Dipping into his rucksack, Keegan produced the shield and then looked curiously at Lascana.

'Thanks, Uncle Keegan,' shouted Aridain, hugging him soundly then disappearing into the kitchen to emerge a few moments later swinging his wooden sword.

'Come on, Chipper, let's go and fight monsters.'

Lascana watched her son with affection and pride as he ran into the woods, giggling, with Chipper barking and bounding along beside him. He was a mischievous boy, to be sure, but also imaginative. 'Don't go too far and keep Chipper with you at all times.'

She turned to Keegan, 'You're as bad as Alfic,' she admonished. 'He'll only expect more next time. But thank you, you're a good friend,' she said, kissing him on the cheek.

'Well, he is my favourite nephew.'

'He's your only nephew,' confirmed Lascana.

'A nephew with yet another trick up his sleeve. Lascana, there's no way he could have known.'

Looking puzzled and staring anxiously towards the woodland beyond, Lascana said, 'Mind reading? Are you sure? There are very few pupils at the school who can do that.'

'No, but Aridain repeated my thoughts word-for-word,' frowned Keegan. 'Anyway, must be going, fish to catch, rabbits to cull, pests to eradicate.'

'OK; bye, Keegan,' Lascana chuckled pensively. 'And thank you.'

Scurrying over to the barn, she scanned the floor anxiously for any more furry invaders. She then quickly collected the hastily discarded wood before dashing back to the cottage and stacking the wood beside the stove.

Trying to confine Aridain to the cottage was like trying to bottle a tornado. He was too much like his father; he needed to be out experiencing the world. Cavorting through the woods, chasing butterflies or running care free across the fields, he constantly returned with jars full of insects, frogs, small furry mice or rabbits. She was concerned that he kept attracting danger, but smiled as she remembered the time Aridain climbed a tree to escape a disgruntled wild boar; it was just as well that Chipper was with him. On a totally separate afternoon Aridain appeared carrying a young fawn- its legs so long that they dragged along the ground - although the situation resolved itself when the mother appeared at the end of the garden. But what if it had been a wolf cub or, worse still, a bear cub?

Hanging up her apron in the kitchen, she walked up the cottage's narrow stairs to her bedroom and sat down in front of the dresser. Removing her headscarf, she drew a comb through her hair and winced in pain from the deep cut on her arm resulting from a trip earlier. Looking in the mirror at the blood seeping through the arm of her smock, she swore. 'That damned Cabala ball. I'm beginning to wish Alfic hadn't brought it home. Aridain's always leaving it in the most inconvenient of places.'

She wondered if his exceptional reflexes were another symptom of his gift. A gift that Vara had indicated was extraordinary. She knew she shouldn't fret, but the sprites' appearance six years ago during his birth was ever present at the back of her mind. She'd talked to other mothers of their children's gifts; they had never once mentioned forest sprites, attracting animals, or mind reading, for that matter.

Well, he'll be going to school next year and there he'll be taught to look after himself, thought Lascana in an attempt to bolster her insecurity.

She ran her hand through her cascade of light brown hair and concentrated instead on her reflection in the mirror. *The years had been kind,* she thought, *despite the long working hours.* Now, in her early thirties, she had been fortunate that Aridain's birth had not spoiled her figure. It pleased her knowing she was still attractive to the opposite sex, as she often caught men staring after her as she passed them by. It pleased her even more, knowing Alfic felt proud of that fact; 'As long as they keep their hands to themselves,' he always added. Smiling shamelessly at her husband's many comments, Lascana rose to her feet and ran down the stairs for a cloth, but was suddenly pulled up short as a figure appeared in the hallway.

'Vara! You gave me a start. I didn't hear you come in.'

Vara exuded an all-encompassing aura of confidence and neatness, but her hair, which never stayed the same colour and always matched her clothes, was ruffled and dirty, as was her shimmering crimson ankle-length outfit.

'What's happened to you?' exclaimed Lascana.

'It's nothing of concern,' grumbled Vara.

A couple of inches shorter than her, the years had treated Vara well, too. No one would have guessed she was in her late fifties, and Lascana always wondered whether it was due to her potions rather than her genes.

'I heard you cursing, is anything wrong?' Vara asked in that all-knowing tone that annoyed Lascana so much.

'It's nothing. I cut my elbow on Aridain's rocking horse yesterday, that's all.'

'Let me look, dear.'

'I'm fine, really, all it needs is a bandage.'

'Don't worry; I've brought something with me. What sort of grandmother would I be if I couldn't use my talents to help my family?'

'Well then, hurry, or I'll be late opening the store.'

Ignoring Lascana's inquiring look, Vara produced a small glass phial that contained a dark, gloopy paste.

Allowing Vara to tend her cut, Lascana ordered, 'Now Vara, no sweets or treats – I mean it. Aridain's teeth will rot away.'

'I know, dear.'

Lascana knew it was pointless to ask Perak to keep an eye on Vara, as Perak was too reserved and worried about upsetting his spouse, unlike Lascana, who had learned to stick up for herself. Besides, Vara never listened to a word he said, anyway.

'Aridain's playing in the woods,' she shouted as she hurried to the front gate.

'My grandson will be fine; I'll tell Perak to go find him. Now go.'

CHAPTER THREE

DARK ARIDAIN

His voice echoing through the woods, Perak shouted, 'Aridain, Aridain!'

'Grand Pop, Grand Pop, we have something to show you,' called Aridain, emerging from the undergrowth with Chipper following closely by.

'Have you, now? Then we'd best have a look, hadn't we?'

'And I picked these for Grandma,' said Aridain, launching himself at Perak and presenting him with a handful of bluebells. Then, wriggling from his arms, Aridain took his hand and, together with Chipper, led him further into the woods through the multi-coloured wild flowers that carpeted the woodland floor.

Ever since Alfic had moved into the cottage, Perak had envied his son and had visited often. He enjoyed walking and discussing the wildlife with Alfic and Lascana, imparting his wisdom to Aridain. There was always something new to learn or see, from the smallest creatures to the largest, with Aridain asking more questions than he could possibly answer. He had always wanted to share with Aridain the magic of the woodland and its creatures, as he had with Alfic before him. As for Vara and their other two children, their no-nonsense, possession driven attitudes had blinded them to the world's true riches.

Smiling proudly, he watched his grandson as he revelled in the world around him and soaked up everything they taught him, just like a sponge. Vara thought it a waste of time walking in the countryside, choosing instead to gather her information from books. Her ingredients were either grown in the garden or purchased from markets and shops, so she never experienced the wonder of the woods or the down lands.

They passed a familiar pond where echo bugs called (now swollen with eggs), and mayflies bobbed up and down from the surface of the water. Nearby a large hornbeam grew with a dark leaved climber winding its way up through the branches, sprouting the purple and yellow flowers of the deadly nightshade plant.

'Look at these, Grand Pop,' shouted Aridain; ever inquisitive, poking a stick at several large dull brown flowers growing uniformly up a thick stem on the woodland floor.

'Be careful of them!' Perak warned loudly.

Aridain dropped his poking stick as Chipper, sniffing them cautiously, backed away instinctively.

'That's a burdock orchid; any disturbance will trigger those flowers to launch nasty looking seeds into the air. Their barbs can be very painful penetrating the eyes, ears and nose and, if left, will work their way into your body.'

'Then what, Grand Pop?'

'Let's just say they cause all sorts of problems. Some people have even died,' said Perak, peering around the woods thoughtfully. 'No doubt your grandma has many uses for their seeds,' he indicated dryly. 'Come on, you were going to show me something.'

Pushing through a small encompassing stand of flowering hazel trees, Perak stopped at the edge of a beautiful sunlit grove and stared in wonder. The woodland floor was covered in the amethyst and blue of early purple orchids, bluebells and the red, yellow and white flowers of climbing honeysuckle. Amongst this beauty, however, was a spectacle Perak had never expected to see. In the centre, male woodland sprites were performing their ritual mating flights, dancing and cavorting amidst the rays of spring sunshine filtering through the trees, while the females hovered close to the ground around what appeared to be a cherry tree seedling growing from the old dead stump.

'Look Grand Pop, isn't it wonderful?'

With tears in his eyes, he turned to Aridain. 'A seedling! I thought the sprites would leave after the old tree died,' whispered Perak. 'Thank you, Aridain, thank you for showing me this; you too, Chipper,' he said, rubbing the faithful dog's head.

'That's alright, Grand Pop; we knew you'd like it.'

In the past he had often walked to the flower-covered copse with Alfic, Aridain and Chipper revelling in the grove's magic. Sensing the old cherry tree's demise, he had warned against chopping it down for fear of upsetting the magical creatures that lived in and around the clearing. However, the previous spring no new flowers had emerged from the ancient trees' deep red branches and examining the trunk they could sense no life within.

'I've decided to make a rocking horse for Aridain from the wood, plus a few useful things for Lascana,' Alfic had commented while sat in front of the fire later that evening.

'The wood spirits are very particular, you know,' said Perak.

'Father, the tree's dead.'

'I know you don't share my values but...'

'Don't worry, I'll be sympathetic.'

The next day, accompanied by Lascana, they had returned with a horse and cart and, after a short thank-you speech to the wood spirits, had taken the tree down. It had taken them several trips, but eventually after a day's sawing and chopping they had transported the wood back to the cottage.

Smiling, Perak thought: *In retrospect it now seems that the very act of felling the old tree had initiated the growth of the seedling.*

Stirred from his musings, Perak squatted to the woodland floor and, examining a dark stain, exclaimed, 'What's this? It looks like a small footprint, and there are more of them across the grove. I've never seen anything like this before – the stain appears to be killing the vegetation.' Then looking up and holding on to Chipper's collar, he whispered fiercely, 'Aridain, what are you doing? Come back here!'

But it was too late; Aridain was already skipping across the clearing through the waist-high flowers.

'It's alright, Grand Pop, they said it's fine.'

Perak's fears were unfounded, however, as the female sprites joined the males in a spiralling dance as Aridain skipped and hopped around the old stump from which the sapling grew.

Watching in astonishment, Perak thought back to Cantlock, the village of his birth, and the magical

Pronghorn Woods to the north, which as a child he had often visited and walked among the various creatures. He had always felt blessed that they allowed him even that, yet here was his grandson doing that very same thing with the creatures' blessing; it seemed the bond forged at his birth had not diminished. Perak realised just how special their grandson was as he danced with these creatures. It saddened him, however, to think that in these beautiful surroundings, where there were no politics or power struggles, just the rhythms of nature, the one thing that was constant in reality was change and Aridain would eventually have to face life's reality; it was the way of things.

At that moment, a shiver ran down his spine, and Perak looked up apprehensively, studying the overhanging canopy. The trees rocked, seemingly in revulsion, as a sudden gust of icy wind shook the surrounding branches. He looked down at a tug on his shirt.

'My friends say it's time to hide. Something nasty is coming, Grand Pop,' said Aridain.

'Yes, I think they're right,' said Perak, scanning their surroundings uneasily. He looked at Chipper. 'Come on, boy.'

Taking Aridain's hand, he retraced their steps as the woods all around fell silent and the atmosphere began to darken. Grasping Aridain's hand even tighter, Perak picked up his pace, his senses alert to the strange and unnatural ambience that pervaded the woods. Jumping on to tree roots and grassy tussocks, they made their way along the path that ran parallel to the stream, back through the marshy area and pond containing the echo bugs. Instinct, or it could have been acute awareness, caused Perak to look up as, with a crack, a branch split loose from above.

'Aridain, look out!'

Grabbing his grandson, Perak leapt to the side as the large branch crashed down across the path. Helping Aridain to his feet, fear gripped him as Chipper growled ominously and he stared in astonishment at a small, child-like figure that stepped on to the path from behind a thick ash tree trunk; its footfalls in the grass, where it brushed against foliage and grasped tree trunks, leaving dark cancerous stains. He realised, without knowing how, that it was this that had spooked the animals in the woods earlier, and now caused him to freeze in fear. The small, stooped figure seemed to be coated in dull, black treacle and its undulating skin, instead of reflecting light, seemed to soak it up as though attempting to suck the warmth from the world.

'Grand Pop, it looks just like me,' said a fascinated Aridain.

Despite his fear, Perak peered closer. Recoiling in shock, he said apprehensively, 'Yes, it does.' Then, ushering Aridain behind him, he backed away slowly.

'What is it, Grand Pop?'

'What are you, and why do you look like my grandson?' he demanded.

Through a dark tangle of straw-like hair, the Dark Creature opened its maw to reveal a mouth full of razor-sharp incisor teeth. 'Grraannddfffaatthherrr, Brrotthhherrrr.'

'What do you mean, "Grandfather"? I'm not your grandfather, and Aridain certainly is not your brother.'

Suddenly the creature shambled towards them with spindly arms outstretched and, opening its maw once more, emitted a mournful, ear-piercing shriek.

'Gggrrraaaandddfathherrrr.'

'Aridain, no!'

Perak watched in horror as Aridain's and the Dark Creature's hands touched. There was a resounding thump and a muted flash; suddenly, Perak felt himself tumbling through the air. Before he blacked out, he felt the stream's frigid waters close over him.

Smoothing out her dress and dabbing at the cut on her elbow, Lascana hurried down the lane as a yellowhammer chanted 'a little bit of bread and no cheese'. The resident blackbird, its breath clearly visible in the crisp spring air, flicked its tail in warning before hopping on to the fence beside the lane and flying noisily into the wood opposite. The reason for the warning call soon became clear as a stoat, gazing about cautiously, scampered on to the stone-built bridge in front of her, then, eyeing up a juicy bug, leapt into the air and caught it in its jaws before scampering quickly back to the stream bank.

Lascana loved this time of year, the time of renewal; it always thrilled her, filling her with anticipation and expectation.

She stopped, suddenly realising that stoat had caught a hornet fly. She knew that hornet flies regularly appeared during the spring, building their hives in dark overhangs. The bridge was dark, and it overhung the stream. Keegan had warned her that they swarmed and attacked at the slightest provocation. Now Lascana had to cross the stone-built bridge without arousing their anger. Treading quietly, she started across the bridge, but something buzzed next to her ear and she panicked. Abandoning all thoughts of stealth, she bolted across the bridge. When she was far enough away, she chanced a look over her shoulder and, confidant that none of the red and yellow assassins were chasing her, slowed to a walk. Alfic always tried his best to explain that the worst thing you can do is panic. 'Think logically,' he always said, but when it came to creepy crawly things and, for that matter, rats, her logic flew away on the wings of fright. She turned at the sound of laughter and spotted two familiar faces sat amongst sacks of barley seed on the back of a horse-drawn hay wagon.

'Morning, Lascana.'

Lascana looked up to see Elgin, a bright, young, up-coming farm labourer and an understudy of Alfic's. With him and slightly older was Nailer Tadman, who studied her casually while chewing on thick slices of meat, cheese and bread.

'Aren't you supposed to be doing something useful? Like work?' she said sarcastically.

'Yes, but we're always up for a bit of light entertainment,' chuckled Nailer.

Ignoring their teasing, her encounter with the flies forgotten; she turned right at the top of the field and continued along the track. Either side of her were extensive field systems, and before her, towering above the row of ancient copper beech and sweet chestnut trees, was the dark, iron-stoned complex of Pellagrin's school shining in the crisp morning sun, founded almost eight hundred years ago by the wizard of the same name. Situated in the province of Durbah in the realm of Aymara, the school with its various buildings, towering domes, battlements and spires was said to be imbued with everlasting magic. Not only was it the oldest centre of learning in Durbah, but as Lascana knew, having studied history, Pellagrin's was also totally self-sufficient. Its grounds comprised the cottage, various outhouses, stables and a farm. The farm consisted of sheep-shearing and milking sheds, pigsties, a dove-cote and chicken coops, plus facilities for cider making. There was also an allotment system, large plant houses, a large rabbit warren, orchards, a fish farm, water-driven mill and large herds of oxen and sheep.

Closing the second of two gates behind her that separated the fields and orchards from the school proper, Lascana gazed to her left having passed the row of magnificent sweet chestnut trees, now dressed in their fresh new greens of spring, as teachers and students busily set up rows of archery targets; while others tied up straw-stuffed warriors for jousting and spear practice.

'Lascana!'

She smiled as her husband ran down the track towards her. 'Alfic, there you are.'

His mane of thick, black hair complementing his ruggedly handsome face, he returned her smile in that cheeky way of his, his dark brown eyes glinting with that hint of mischievousness that she loved so much. 'Don't tell me, you'll be late again tonight?'

'The lambs are coming thick and fast,' he apologised. 'Hey, it's not such a bad thing, as long as I keep the school

supplied with meat and veg for their tables, the powers
that be leave us alone. Personally, that suits me down to
the ground. I'll try to finish earlier tomorrow.'

'Don't make promises you can't keep.'

He kissed her soundly on the lips. 'I'll see you later.'

As he disappeared around the corner of one of the
large plant houses, she smiled to herself; *He certainly was
a man of many talents.*

Now in his thirties he had mellowed since his army
days but had lost none of his good sense. Kind and
generous to a fault, Alfic was a very good friend if the
cause was just and right, defending his friends and family
to the death. However, he could also be short-tempered
when it came to any form of injustice, and if you didn't
pull your weight, or you were up to no good, he was a
rolling cloud of thunder.

Someone barged her aside, and she looked up abruptly.

'Hey woman! Watch who you're shoving!' admonished
a teenager, smiling conspiratorially with three of his
friends. He was dressed in the white and purple robes of a
Demonology apprentice. 'Stop day-dreaming and attend
to your duties; some of us want to make something of our
lives.'

'Sorry! Stuck up, little grunt,' she hissed. 'It's not as
though I did it on purpose.' *I don't know…* she thought,
*most students accept their newfound status with honour and
humility, while some become quite insufferable and
big-headed.*

Hurrying along the path, she passed the old defensive
wall with its grass covered earthen bank. On top of this
grew a row of stately, grey-barked pines that towered

above a tightly clipped hazel hedge. Also built against the earthen bank were the soldiers' barracks and rows of stables.

Then strolling across the grass underneath Pellagrin's oak, she joined the circular cobbled roadway that serviced the small one-roomed structures arranged around the courtyard used as shops (one of which she rented). Also situated here were the living quarters, kitchens and the old fortress that now housed the administration rooms and Wizards' quarters.

'Lascana, you sexy minx, come here and give me a hug.'

'Mace!' beamed Lascana. 'We've missed you. How's the war?'

'Sooner or later, those miniscule munchkins will have to surrender. It's just a matter of when.'

Disengaging from his vice-like grasp, she mused, 'It's strange that the darklings attacked in the first place. After all, we promised to leave them in peace and they must have realised they could never win.'

'Who knows what goes through a "Bitterlings" mind? So, how's that good-for-nothing husband of yours?' asked Mace cheerily.

'Still as busy as ever.'

'And that good-for-nothing gamekeeper? Still causing trouble, is he?'

'Keegan's fine. He sends his love,' teased Lascana.

'Love! When you see him, tell him I'll box his ears, he still owes me money from our last card game.'

'Tell him yourself.'

Lascana looked at Mace hopefully, 'Have you spoken to my father?'

'Yes, Colonel Taro sends his love, and he wanted me to give you this letter.'

'How is he?'

'He's fine, he looks in great shape for a man in his fifties and yes, as usual, he's in the thick of things.'

'Did he say anything about coming home?'

'I'm sorry, darlin, he said nothing to me, only to tell you he's happy, and he's alright.'

Lascana took the worn envelope. As long as she had known her father, he had been in the army fighting one enemy or another, and he'd made no secret of the fact that he preferred life in the army to life at home, that he coveted danger and adventure. Over many long years, he had worked his way up through the ranks until he had reached the lofty position of colonel. Colonel Taro, an achievement he was very proud of, not that it made any difference to his wife or three daughters. Apart from the healthy dowry money their mother received, they sat at home waiting to hear the news that he had been permanently injured or killed. She worried constantly that Aridain might have inherited some of those traits.

Smiling resolutely, she said, 'Aridain will be thrilled you're back, he often asks after you.'

Rubbing at his shoulder, Mace said, 'Yes, I've missed the little mite; he's always a very attentive listener.'

'Too attentive, we can never get him to sleep after you've left, filling his head with your campaigns and adventures.'

In his early thirties, wearing his worn, crimson leather armour and his grey iron sword strapped to his back, Mace looked every inch an army captain and a seasoned campaigner. He was also a member of an ancient order called the Greyswords; highly skilled warriors sworn to protect the school against any and all forms of magic and incursion. That he'd actually survived this long unscathed was a tribute to his extraordinary skill in the field of battle. Sporting light brown curly hair and dark brown eyes, he had the rugged good looks that Lascana still found attractive. She had actually dated the big handsome weapons master, but as friendly and fun loving as he was, his reckless love for danger and adventure had ruled him out as a reliable father.

'Are you alright, you look uncomfortable?'

'I picked up an infection fighting those cursed darklings. Now and then it flares up. It just won't go away,' bemoaned Mace, struggling to scratch the spot beneath his armour.

'Don't scratch it, you'll only make it worse. Go and see Alsike, I know of several soldiers who have returned from the wilds with the same thing and they all went to the school's healer.'

'Oh, I don't know... I'm not a great fan of enchantments.'

'Oh, don't be a baby, for an army hero you are squeamish sometimes, Captain Mace Denobar.'

'I'm awake,' coughed Perak, looking around frantically. 'Aridain, it's all right, you can stop shouting at me now.'

'You wouldn't wake up Grand Pop. I had to hold your head out of the water,' said Aridain tearfully, 'so you wouldn't drown.'

'Are you alright?' exclaimed Perak, recalling the events that led to their dilemma.

'Just very wet and cold,' said Aridain, standing up in the water that lapped at his waist. 'A voice in my head said, "protect your grandfather or he'll die", so I did. Are you all right now, Grand Pop?' asked Aridain.

'I'll be fine. A voice you say; anyone we know?'

Aridain shook his head.

'Where's the creature?' gasped Perak.

'Gone. It stood on the bank for a long time, then left. I think I hurt it.'

'What do you mean?'

'It wasn't happy, it was moaning.'

'Where's Chipper?'

Aridain shook his head again, and tears began to stream down his cheeks once more.

'I'm sure he's fine,' said Perak encouragingly, but as he tried to stand up, he gasped with pain.

Seeing the concern on Aridain's troubled face, he said, 'Don't fret, now, it's nothing. We must get you home into the warm before that thing returns, then we'll have a word with your grandmother. Maybe she can shed some light on what's happened.'

Just then they heard barking and, moments later, Chipper appeared on the bank, quickly followed by Vara.

'Grandma, Chipper,' shouted Aridain gleefully.

'Aridain, are you alright?'

'Yes, Grandma,' shouted Aridain, 'but Grand Pop's hurt.'

'What did you do now, Perak Bruin? What happened?' she snapped. 'I can't trust you with anything...'

'Are you going to continue raving, or are you going to help us? Find a place for us to climb out.'

'I've a good mind to leave you down there.' Vara looked around. 'Well, this bough is blocking the path; you'll never climb out here.' And, muttering under her breath, Vara disappeared upstream. 'Here,' she hollered, her voice echoing through the woods, 'you can climb out here.'

Splashing upstream through knee high water, Perak led Aridain to a section of the bank where the roots of a holly tree were exposed to the air.

'You first, Aridain,' said Perak, pushing him up the bank.

'It's alright, Grand Pop, I can do it,' and, like a mountain goat, Aridain pulled himself up the bank. When he reached the top, he turned around and, together with Vara, helped Perak scramble up and over the edge.

Seeing the concern in Aridain's eyes, Perak said, 'Come on, don't worry now, it's only a bruise.'

Vara, who had been studying Perak's sweating, deathly pale skin, said, 'I don't think so. Here, let me see.' Grasping his shoulder firmly, Vara examined it. She then looked at Aridain, shivering in his wet clothing.

'So, is someone going to tell me what happened?'

'Something attacked us. It looked just like me but with long spidery arms and legs; it looked like a piece of liquorice and had horrible yellow eyes,' said Aridain excitedly. 'It made that branch fall on top of us, Grandma, then, when it tried to get Grand Pop, I protected him, but we fell into the stream, that's how Grand Pop hurt his shoulder. Grand Pop was very brave.'

'Hmmm, is that so? Come on, let's get out of the woods and back to the cottage.'

Their breath now clearly visible in the cold of spring's late afternoon, Perak scanned the trees, searching the sun-dappled woodland as Vara ushered Aridain along the path and back through the trees. But there was no sign of the strange creature.

Emerging from Farend wood into the lane, they approached the cottage.

'When we get indoors, Aridain, change out of those clothes and get warm by the fire, while I see to your grandfather.'

Perak gratefully complied as Vara helped him inside, out of the cold wind, and led him into the kitchen. Now in her element, Vara sat him down and began to clean the wound on his scalp. 'So, are you going to tell me what really happened?' she demanded.

Perak smiled weakly and shrugged. 'Aridain's telling the truth. This thing, whatever it was, looked just like him, although it was nothing like Aridain. It was as black as night, hostile, and when it stared at me it felt like cold daggers piercing my heart. I wanted to run in the opposite direction but I couldn't.'

'It looked like Aridain, you say,' said Vara who, having dressed Perak's head wound, began carefully prodding and probing Perak's shoulder.

'Yes, but his opposite; I sensed only malice. Aridain stepped in front of me as this thing reached out,' gasped Perak. 'It's strange. It totally ignored Aridain and looked at me in puzzlement, longing even; it called me

Grandfather and Aridain Brother.' Perak looked up at Vara intently. 'Aridain said the thing watched from the bank as I lay unconscious, but never approached. He said it looked "sad".'

'Does this hurt?' Vara manipulated his arm, and Perak cried out. 'I'll take that as a yes.' Then, examining his shoulder again, Vara announced, 'You've dislocated your shoulder, you silly man.'

'I didn't do it on purpose.'

'I wouldn't put it past you. I'll have to pop it back in.'

'I do believe you'll have to touch me to do that,' he said ironically. 'Twice in one day. I can't remember the last time; I think it was when you had to apply that poultice to a bump on my head nearly a year ago to the day; after you threw that book at me if I remember correctly,' he said, knowing that Vara tried desperately to avoid situations like this, as they made her extremely uncomfortable.

Exhausted, Perak watched as Vara turned and fished around in her bag of potions, tonics and concoctions; a bag Perak was sure was bigger on the inside. She then mixed the ingredients together on a chopping board, pouring the mixture into a glass of weak beer.

'I think the knock on your head is affecting your common sense,' stated Vara.

He smiled, despite the pain. 'If this is the only way I can get some attention, then perhaps I'll injure myself more often.'

'That can be arranged; now, drink this; it will help dull the pain and your pitiable attempts at affection.'

'Tastes good, what's in it?' he slurred.

'It's a concentrated poppy and hop mixture if you must know,' she stated casually, and then, waiting for the sedative to take effect, said, 'OK, I'm going to count to three.'

'OK.'

'One.' Suddenly, without warning, Vara grabbed his shoulder and pulled. Unprepared and so relaxed was Perak that he hardly felt any pain.

'What happened to two and three?'

'Nothing. I just didn't use them. Anything else?'

'What?'

'Did anything else happen?'

'Yes. Aridain said a voice spoke to him, told him to protect me. Do you have any idea what he's talking about, Vara?' asked Perak. 'Has this creature or have today's events anything to do with Aridain's birth?'

'I'm not sure. I'll have to look into it.'

'That's what you said six years ago.' Watching his wife intently, he asked, 'Vara, what aren't you telling me? OK, fine; I'll tell you what I think. I think this is the same thing that terrified the animals in the wood earlier today. I also think this creature does have something to do with Aridain's birth, which puts our grandson in danger.'

'Then what are you asking me for? It seems you've got it all worked out.'

'Vara!' snapped Perak.

'I take it that until I tell you, you won't let this drop.'

'Very perceptive.'

Vara took a deep breath. 'On the night of Aridain's birth, after you left, an apparition appeared; the apparition of the Dragon Lord Pellagrin. He confirmed what I suspected.'

'Pellagrin's ghost?'

'Yes, can I continue?'

Perak nodded irritably.

'He said our grandson is the Elemental of Light, the Balefire Taal.'

'An apparition of Pellagrin told you our grandson is something called a Balefire Taal.'

'Yes. A being that is destined to destroy the Firebrand stone and find the Chimera stone. Only this time he has been tasked to destroy them both, in order to bring balance to the world.'

'Vara, have you been sniffing black orchid vapour? First of all, Pellagrin has been dead eight hundred years and, secondly, the stones are a myth.'

Shaking her head in consternation, Vara said, 'That attitude is the very reason I never told you or anyone else.'

'You must admit, it is pretty far-fetched. Although there's a sect of witches based in Durbah called the Balefires,' mused Perak.

Ignoring him, Vara continued. 'That same night I travelled to the school. I found ancient scrolls that confirmed it. There's something else, and you're not going to like this. As well as an Elemental of light there is also a Dark Elemental, born at the exact same time, both are destined to do battle.'

'The creature in the wood,' declared Perak.

'Yes.'

'Great, so you're telling me that somehow our grandson has to find these stones, destroy them and kill this creature?'

'And there's more.'

'Of course there is!'

'Once they are destroyed, the Dark Creature will have no purpose.'

'And die?'

'Yes.'

'And Aridain?'

Vara looked away so as Perak wouldn't see her tears. 'He'll have no purpose either; it is the price to be paid.'

Perak, struggling to digest Vara's words, said, 'You're serious.'

Wiping at her eyes, Vara replied with as much conviction as she could muster. 'Pellagrin's spirit said, "between us he stands more than an even chance." Now, with your help, he stands an even better one.'

Sitting suddenly upright, Perak exclaimed, 'that's it! Aridain said a voice in his head told him to protect me. Did the spirit touch Aridain in any way?'

'Before Pellagrin disappeared, he touched Aridain's forehead.'

'Are you certain of this?'

Vara replied impatiently. 'Yes. Why?'

'I think he's still here,' he said, pointing to his temple. 'Inside Aridain's head, that's what he meant when he said, "with our protection he stands more than an even chance".'

'So, what are you saying?'

'The reason for his presence could be twofold; one for protection, and the other for strength when the time to destroy the stones finally arrives. I remember hearing of a spell involving infusing another's spirit with a living person that accomplishes the very same thing.'

'How would you know of such a thing?'

'I'm good friends with the head of the school, Almagest, remember? So do Lascana and Alfic know?' asked Perak, 'About Aridain?'

Vara turned towards him and said curtly, 'No, and they don't need to, nor do his friends, for I would not like to see the trouble it would cause him through jealousy and envy. No need to thrust these burdens on a small child before his time.'

Sat in the warm kitchen in front of the range, his wife's infusion now working its magic, Perak watched lethargically as Vara made up an arm sling from a piece of sacking and tied it around his arm. He then allowed her to lead him into the small but cosy living room and sit him in front of the fire. The last thing he felt was a blanket being draped over his body before he fell into a deep sleep.

Now that Perak was asleep, Vara looked around the sparsely furnished living room then, making her way into the small kitchen, sighed in exasperation at the simple, primitive surroundings. Why did Alfic not want to better himself? Why couldn't he have some ambition, like his brother and sister? They were next in line to succeed Head Teachers Almagest and Exedra at the school. With her guidance, Alfic would have one day made a fine gentleman wizard in line for the Sivan council. Instead, he was turning into his father, whose only ambition in life was to work in the dirt and clean up after animals. Lascana could be a lady of standing instead of a common shopkeeper. And yet, Perak's close relationship with Magen and Alfic was something she never had. She shook her head, perplexed. *Perhaps Perak is right, if things had been different; had I not pushed them so hard, perhaps my children would have been less resentful of their mother.* As things stood, she and Alfic were barely on speaking terms, while Magen, who she'd never empathised with, deliberately kept her distance. And now her youngest son, Kuelack, once her pride and joy, had become a sadistic bully.

Vara looked down at Chipper, who stared back expectantly with ears raised, and scratched his forehead. 'You don't know how lucky you are, Chipper; families, relationships, nothing but a burden. They argue but never listen, only focusing on their own petty troubles instead of focusing on the long term. All you worry about is your next meal and finding a stick to play with. You saw the creature, didn't you? No doubt it scared you too.' Returning to the kitchen, she made sure the range was burning brightly, then fed Chipper a small slice of meat. 'Go on, go see Aridain, he's asleep upstairs.'

Watching the Doberman sprint from the kitchen and bound noisily up the stairs, her thoughts turned to the dilemma that was her grandson, and what the appearance of the strange creature represented. At the time of his birth, she remembered gently holding the newly born Aridain in her arms, feeling pride at the primeval energy surging from him up through her arms and into her body. She sensed his power, a power she had never felt in a child before.

Since his birth she had believed there would be enough time to prepare Aridain, to teach him to control his power. Now Perak's words confirmed her worst fears; The

Dark Taal had sought out her grandson, and his power had led it right to Aridain.

She opened her bag of potions and remedies and produced several herbs and powders, spreading them out across the kitchen's surface. Her mind awhirl with theories, she turned her attention to mixing her concoctions ready for her clients the next day.

CHAPTER FOUR

CHALK AND CHEESE

Resplendent in his pleated black and crimson bodice, trousers and sequined cloak, Kuelack strode purposefully down the opulent west wing corridor situated on the third floor of the old keep, fondling the clasp of Second Wizard. The clasp awarded him instant respect from everyone except the Sivan Council, which consisted of Almagest the school's headmaster, Exedra the joint head of the school, himself and his sister Magen.

'Kuelack, Kuelack!'

'What is it, Sister?' complained Kuelack impatiently, as Magen's familiar voice filled the corridor, turning and looking towards her with piercing grey eyes. It was a look that filled his students and many of the teachers with trepidation.

'Did you feel it?' she whispered, striding purposefully beside him. 'You must have felt it!'

'Of course.'

'Whatever the magic was, it was close. Almagest and Exedra are furious. They promised there would be serious consequences for whoever's dabbling,' said Magen, dumbfounded.

'As we knew they would,' he replied matter-of-factly. 'So, what's the official story?'

'Until otherwise decreed, it was the work of an unqualified student.'

'Really,' mused Kuelack, glancing deliberately at his sister from beneath thin angular eyebrows, 'although I doubt any of the senior teachers will believe that.'

'You know, if you fondle that necklace too much, you'll go blind,' teased Magen.

Staring down at the badge of office draped around his neck, comprising a roaring Firedrake motif, backed by a red dragon with outstretched wings, Kuelack said seriously, 'This symbol is no laughing matter; I have sacrificed much to attain the respect it grants me.'

'I know it's what you've always strived for, but that badge doesn't magically remove your sense of humour. What I mean is, do you have to be so serious all the time, especially with me?'

Kuelack studied his sister, who, in her mid-thirties, looked regal in her crimson and turquoise free-flowing dress and headband, but she was not beautiful; *She isn't even good looking,* he thought.

A 'Plain Jane', she was a younger version of their mother, Vara, sporting tumbling locks of dark brown hair and the same dark brown eyes. She would have made an excellent Head Sorceress if it weren't for the fact that she'd inherited many of their father's idiotic qualities. She often argued that he should try to see his father and elder brother for what they were, rather than disregard them because of the way they chose to live. "It takes all sorts to make a world," was her favourite saying.

They turned from the beautifully furnished red-carpeted corridor with portrait-hung walls and descended the main stairway to the ground floor. As they stepped from the stairway, Magen's closest friend, Beria Dearing, accompanied by Ramus, the school's expert on dragon lore, hailed them. Beria was dressed in the white robes of a teacher, the collar and belt of which were embroidered with a lit candle motif. Her cuffs, drawn back hood and white thick Argol wool gorget were all edged in turquoise; the colour and the motif signifying she was a teacher of witchcraft. Ramus wore the same white uniform, but it was edged in dark flame red and embroidered with dragon's heads on his collar and belt.

The pair could not be more different, thought Kuelack; Beria was short and slight and Ramus, at nearly seven feet, was tall and rangy. Beria had a soft, rounded face framed in long auburn hair tied at the neck and Ramus, sporting a dark, neatly cropped beard, moustache and hair framing a long face and thin-lipped mouth, looked dark and severe.

'Good morning Magen, Kuelack,' said Beria, the pair inclining their heads respectfully. 'Unusual for an assembly to be called at such short notice, don't you think?'

'I'm sure our esteemed leader will explain everything in the Assembly Hall,' replied Kuelack dryly.

'Don't be modest Kuelack, you can air your views, you're with friends,' said Ramus in his deep rich voice, 'after all, to those of us who know what we're looking for, it's plainly obvious that things are not as they appear.'

'Is there something you wish to say, Ramus?' dared Kuelack.

'No; merely speculating on the recent turn of events.'

Eyeing them strangely, Beria said, 'Well, I agree with Ramus, there is more to this gathering than meets the eye.'

'And speculation and guesswork won't help.' Studying the ornate, coving, mouldings, tapestries and paintings hanging at various points on the wall, Kuelack, in an attempt to change the subject said, 'The school has a proud history, don't you think?'

'Yes, it does, but the violence is a part of the school's history best forgotten; we live in a more civilised society now,' retorted Magen.

'The school was fighting for its life, Sister, violence to counter violent aggressors.'

'Still, best those days never return, Brother.'

'It was those days that made this school great, Magen.'

In silence, Kuelack together with Magen, Beria and Ramus strode purposefully across the hall and along the corridors of their home, teachers and assistants nodding to them as they went about their daily routines, scurrying back and forth, servicing the requirements of the school seven days a week - like a vivacious colony of ants servicing an ever-demanding queen. Some carried mysterious objects, others important manuscripts, while more junior members of staff hurried around, weighed down with arms full of books or dragging heavy wooden boxes noisily across the floor, to the displeasure of studying senior luminaries.

'When I look around now, all I see is apathy and bureaucracy! A dose of chaos now and then can be a good thing; it shakes things up, concentrates people's thoughts, and makes us stronger. Tell me, Sister, Beria, would you use your gifts to fight for this school, protect its legacy?'

Magen turned on him in indignation. 'Are you suggesting we return to those barbaric ways?'

'Of course not, I'm merely curious.'

'If my history serves me correctly, it took Pellagrin, and then wizard Rueben, almost two hundred years to bring peace to these parts,' said Beria.

'It was a grave mistake if you ask me, refurbishing the building,' said Kuelack, looking up at the ornate roof, the glazed quarter rail windows and the discretely covered murder holes. 'They should have kept it as an open courtyard.'

'My, we are in a morose mood today, Brother, all this talk of conflict and dark days long gone.'

'That's your brother all over,' mumbled Ramus offhandedly.

Walking in awkward silence between tall, neatly trimmed bay trees, sweet smelling wallflowers and colourful borders encompassed by neatly tended lawns, more teachers and staff joined them on the path as they funnelled towards the Hall of Worship that led from the Assembly Hall.

'I've always liked those gargoyles,' said Ramus suddenly.

Starting from his thoughts, Kuelack hissed. 'What are you babbling about now?'

'The statues scattered around the school. They're Albacores, native to Zapata, they remind me of my home. They were fashioned with Albacore blood, allegedly. It's said, Kuelack, that they come alive if dark magic is used against the school.'

'Twaddle and fantasy, Ramus.'

'What is wrong with the pair of you today?' asked Magen, eyeing them fixedly.

Revelling in his small victory, Kuelack entered the spacious assembly hall and, accompanied by Magen, walked to the front of the hall between the rows of benches. Then they climbed the marbled steps to join the joint heads of the school, Almagest and Exedra already seated at the higher council table on the raised stage, while Ramus and Beria peeled off into the galleried seating area.

Nodding respectfully, Kuelack said guardedly, 'Exedra, Almagest.'

'Kuelack,' replied Almagest, seriously.

'Nice of you two to join us… finally,' said Exedra, glaring at them.

Ignoring Exedra's derisive comment, Kuelack sat on Exedra's right, behind the long ornate wooden desk while Magen sat on Almagest's left. Watching the teachers take to their seats amid noisy murmuring, he couldn't help but notice the immodest stares of the men he knew were attracted to the single, powerful joint head of the school. He couldn't say he blamed them; nearly one hundred-and thirty-years Almagest's junior. With long, flowing blond hair, finely chiselled features and a figure accentuated by a figure-hugging white gown, Exedra's beauty turned the heads of the most devoted men. But he also knew that these suitors were wasting their time as Exedra, proudly displaying the headdress and cross-shaped turquoise badge of office, took her new position very seriously. As the teachers settled down, Almagest, pulling his large, white, crimson-lined hood back from his greying hair and ancient lined and bearded face, rose to his feet. Then, in a deep, resounding voice addressed the assembled teachers.

'Some of you already know the reason we're here, some of you may not. For those who don't, powerful, unrestrained magic has been used on the grounds.' He waited for them to digest the information and the murmuring to die down and then continued, 'Despite the official explanation, this magic's very nature eliminates the students as none possess the knowledge or feral power necessary to have produced its like. So, we can only assume that someone here conjured it or, more worryingly, someone not belonging to this school,' he said gravely.

'Does this represent a threat?' came an inquiry from the assembled teachers.

'We're not sure, but we must investigate magic of this magnitude; we have to establish who would unleash this power and to what end. Let there be no doubt in anyone's mind that we will find the culprit or culprits. Before we start, I will give you all the chance to come forward or surrender any knowledge you may have concerning this disquieting episode.'

Kuelack watched intently as the aged Wizard clasping the red sickle moon design stitched into his silk ankle-length green and brown sash, studied the faces of the gathered Wizards and Sorceresses, his white First Wizard's robe shining brightly as if lit from within.

'Very well, Karnack, disperse your men, please,' said Almagest darkly.

His armour jangling in the silence, the Chief Greysword instructed the guard outside to secure the doors, then instructed his fellow Greyswords, Mace, Vanir and Jackamar, to position themselves inside the exits, their swords drawn and poised point down in front of them, their duty to let no one in or out.

'What is going on here? What's the meaning of this?' shouted a member of the crowd.

'Are we now prisoners?' asked another.

'Until we establish everyone's loyalty, no one will leave the Assembly Hall.'

Almagest then fixed his attention on a small man sat at the front. 'If you would, please, Mass?'

The school's psychic, Mass Martin - his white robes bordered in green but possessing no emblems - slowly looked up then walked solemnly on to the stage to stand in front of the pre-eminent Wizard, his large bald head illuminated by the light streaming in through the vaulted windows overhead as if to accentuate his formidable gift.

'This is an invasion of privacy!' shouted a female voice from the crowd.

'I agree!' objected a gruff male voice. 'Is this really necessary?'

'If you have nothing to hide, then you have nothing to fear,' said Almagest.

'How do we know you're not the cause of this magic? Why don't you go first?'

'Very well; Mass, if you please, scan the four of us first.'

As Kuelack watched Mass concentrate, the hall took on an eerie silence. From the large alcoves in between the stained windows around the hall, the statues of the gods and deities seemed to stare in judgement and antipathy at the outrageous but necessary flaunting of the rules. Shaking his head, Mass then turned to the crowd. 'Please relax; this will take but a moment of your time.'

'This is ridiculous! You two could be working together for all we know.'

'I'm afraid, ladies and gentlemen, you'll just have to trust me,' replied Mass Martin.

The look on each person's face reflected their feelings regarding this intrusion of their minds; most simply endured it, while some stared back in unveiled disgust. When Mass finally looked up, he turned to Almagest and shook his head.

'Thank you, Mass, and thank you all for your patience,' smiled Almagest, slowly sweeping his gaze across the room. 'Keep vigilant and, of course, do not inform the students; the school's routine will go on as it always has. Questions, anyone?'

Kuelack sat serenely scanning the assembled teachers, sensing their unrest.

'No, then that will be all for now. Teachers Kale and Mace, can you stay behind please?'

Kuelack sat quietly as he watched the teachers file out of the Assembly Hall, a self-satisfied smile on his face.

In her high, lyrical voice, Exedra added, 'If we have an outside threat to the school, we must take it seriously.'

A tall, rangy, twenty-one-year-old youth named Kale, the most recent addition to the teachers' ranks, approached the podium together with the muscular weapons master. In his new white brown-bordered robes of Animistic, his collar and belt embossed with an animal's paw impression, Kale, shrinking like a wilting daisy in bright sunlight, pulled back his hood to stare up at the Sivan with clear dark green eyes from a young tanned face, framed by dark brown, shoulder length hair.

'Firstly, the school would like to express its sadness at the untimely death of your mentor, Torsk,' said Almagest sincerely. 'He will be sorely missed.'

'He was a great man.' Kale looked at Almagest gravely. 'I only hope I can justify his and your faith in me.'

'I said nothing to the assembly for fear of causing panic, but we have been receiving reports of a "shadow creature," on the grounds,' said Almagest clearly, looking intently from Mace to the Animistic. 'This thing may have something to do with the magic we've all detected, or it may not; but Kuelack has recommended that you look into it,'

'All the reports have come from in and around Farend Woods,' instructed Kuelack, 'and the area of the stream.' Then, looking meaningfully at Mace, Kuelack said, 'I want you to ascertain any threat from outside the school.'

'As you wish,' replied Mace.

'Then we'll leave it in both of your capable hands,' instructed Almagest.

That night Celias Urkit carefully positioned the noose of his trap across the well-defined deer track that snaked between two sturdy sweet chestnut trees, then wiping his sweating palms on his mud-stained trousers, took a draft from his pocket-sized whisky flask and, looking around cautiously, sat down to wait in the darkness behind a large oak trunk.

He grumbled to himself, 'If that jumped-up overseer thinks I'm going to plead for my job, then he's in for a big surprise: telling me I can't catch game! It's not my fault that the lazy, overstuffed King Pheronis and his castle full of hangers on have scoffed all the wild boar on the estate. I'm not the Goddess Seline who can create animals out of thin air! Well, if I can't earn enough money to eat, I'll just have to take my payment another way.'

Taking another draft from his flask and yawning loudly, the cold night-time breeze caused him to drift in and out of sleep. How long he'd been dozing he couldn't tell, but it wasn't the woodland's familiar night-time noises that woke him but its absence. Feeling suddenly uneasy, he peered between the tree trunks, silhouetted starkly against the frosty ground.

Strange, he thought, *I could have sworn...* He stopped and stared open-mouthed at the small black inky creature that shambled from behind a tree, staring at him from the darkness with dark marbled yellow eyes. An intense fear rooted him to the spot. And when the Dark Creature moved closer, he saw it had the face of a young boy, but that's where its semblance ended. Walking on thin gangly limbs like a Jarawape, its face framed by long dark, reedy hair, it looked thin and undernourished. Steeling himself as best he could, he watched, still rooted to the spot as the 'boy' continued to approach. Petrified, he quaked, 'What the hell are you? It looks as if you were born of a tar pit!' Then, seeing the comprehension on its face, he said more confidently. 'I'll tell you what; when I catch my dinner we can share, ok?'

Nodding slowly, it opened its mouth as if to speak, but instead howled mournfully, revealing a cavernous maw full of sharp fangs.

'Seline preserve us!'

Backing away, his short-lived self-assurance evaporating, Celias Urkit shouted, 'What the hell are you?'

Then, turning in panic, he ran erratically through the trees and woody scrub. Loosing track of time, he fled blindly through the night, his breath coming in short panicked gasps and falling to the frosty floor for the umpteenth time; he turned and looked around in trepidation. When nothing appeared through the frost-covered undergrowth, he heaved a sigh of relief, confident he had lost the terrifying creature.

Alas, he didn't see or hear the Dark Creature's silent attack, as in one fluid movement it leapt from the trees. He screamed as sharp claws pierced his back, his scream cut off as razor-sharp teeth pierced his skull. Powerless to resist, Celias Urkit screamed in silent, agonised terror as the creature sucked his very soul from his body.

CHAPTER FIVE

CONFUSION AND UNCERTAINTY

The following morning, Kale Sim made his way to the stream that wound its way through the school's grounds and began searching the surrounding woodland, in an attempt to verify the report of a strange creature. Having made his way past the gamekeeper's cabin, which sat between the school's two small fish stocked lakes; he followed the stream's course to the water mill, its large oak constructed wheel turning rhythmically in the fog. Kale knocked on the door and Elias Tan, the baker who everyone agreed looked like he could well have been a pirate with his sharp features and dark brooding looks, stepped out from the interior. 'Yes.'

'I'm Kale, the new Animistic's teacher; I'm here regarding the noises you heard.'

'I know who you are, about bloody time. Woke me up again last night and scared me half to death,' said Elias, wiping his flour-covered hands on his long leather apron. 'Sad business about Torsk; nice fella, didn't deserve to die like that.'

'No, no, he didn't,' replied Kale darkly. In an effort to push the conversation forwards, he said, 'The noise, where did you hear it?'

'Down in the hollow, by the stream.'

'Thanks, I'll get right on it.'

'No, thank you; I'm glad someone is taking me seriously. When I tell people what I'm seeing and hearing down here, they think I'm mad.'

'Don't worry, we will deal with it.'

'Any idea what it could be?'

'Mating foxes, it could even be courting Scarrion lizards, Kale lied. 'They can make quite a din.'

'I know what foxes sound like, and that was no fox; Scarrion lizards, not so sure.'

'Have you seen the thing that's making all the noise?' encouraged Kale.

'Well, no, but whatever it is, catch it,' said Elias grimly. 'I don't want it stealing my grain or attacking my horse. Drummer's getting on, you know, the ruckus is scaring him to death.'

'I'll see to it Elias, try not to worry.'

Shaking the baker's hand, he made his way from the mill and, brushing the water from his grey utilitarian cloak, he turned and crossed the ford. Glad to be under cover, sheltered from the constant drizzle that fell from the low oppressive clouds, he entered a stand of flowering hawthorn trees and with head bowed in trepidation, leant trembling against a tree and wiped at his sweaty palms. *If I encounter this thing, will I run in panic?* He then cursed as a hawthorn needle spiked his finger; it was like a slap in the face. *Hold it together Kale, you've been given an important task, you can do this. Think. Figure this out.* At first, he found it hard to focus, but then he recalled his mentor's, (Torsk's), teachings. *Fear is the mind killer, without clarity of mind all you see is the fog of uncertainty. Stumbling around for clarity, no one discovers the truth until it's too late.* Recalling the words sharpened his thought process and cleared his mind.

As Almagest had inferred and his own inquiries had confirmed from the foot and handprints, something was ranging far and wide, leaving a lingering rot on trees, plants and woodland floor, a dark miasma that when touched exuded, and there was no other word for it, evil.

He knew the countryside hadn't always been devoid of large magical creatures such as Harpies, Firedrakes and Griffons. Torsk had taught him that centuries ago, during the human expansion, they had forced many wondrous creatures from their established territories until they left only the tiny benevolent ones, and now even those were scarce. Apart from travelling hundreds of leagues into the wilds, the only way to see these magical creatures now was in travelling carnival acts, or in schools for educational purposes, which made this episode even more unusual, as their loathing for humans was well known. *So why has a large magical creature chosen to come here to the heart of human civilisation?* he thought.

Noticing another spreading dark patch, Kale placed his hand against the small tree trunk. Trying to contain his trepidation, he pushed his hand against the dark rot and concentrated in an attempt to understand it further. An overwhelming lust for blood pervaded his being, together with a violent hunger, dark despair, and a desire; no, not desire, a longing for an object. His mind suddenly besieged, he fell to the damp earth, his world spinning as he struggled to cope with the overwhelming malevolent feeling.

Fool, he thought, *to think that you, Kale, a novice, could comprehend evil such as this.*

He suddenly looked up at a pair of Magpies chattering noisily overhead and, gathering his thoughts, climbed unsteadily to his feet, careful now to avoid the black decay. Eager to escape the cloying stench of evil, Kale continued along the stream bank, picking his way through the wet brush and out into the open beside the familiar line of willows used by the school for coppicing. Through the iron-grey day, beyond the willows, he could just make out the old guard house now turned into a dwelling and occupied by the Bruin family, smoke rising lazily from the chimney into the misty sky and beyond that Farend wood. Leaping over the fence, Kale crossed the bridge and walked into the woods, passing beneath the stand of magnificent Ash trees, the tops of which were obscured by sinuous strands of mist. Sniffing at the damp air, he followed the path, the grass and plants now stained permanently with the creature's passing, probing the trees with his senses in an attempt to distinguish anything that would attract the strange creature.

So why would this creature, whatever it may be, keep returning to Farend Woods? he mused.

It was then that he heard the laughter of a child and the bark of a dog. Pushing his way through a stand of hazel trees hung with catkins, Kale followed the bizarre, happy, babbling sound, then stopped and stared in amazement. Instead of a boy throwing a stick for his dog or playing at sword fighting, he saw a youngster on the garden's periphery, skipping and dancing with a congregation of sprites, pixies and nymphs that bobbed and weaved around his head and shoulders in an elaborate ballet. With a snarl the dog, a large chocolate-coloured Doberman, turned towards him and growled menacingly, and the woodland sprites, so joyous and carefree moments before, fled, disappearing into the surrounding trees.

Unafraid, Kale gazed intently across the clearing at the Doberman. Abruptly it ceased its aggressive behaviour and ran towards him, tail wagging, followed by the boy. 'Hello, my name is Kale; you must be Aridain,' he said, shaking his tiny hand.

'Hello, Mister Kale. How do you know my name?'

'I'm a teacher at the school and I know Keegan and your father, they've told me all about you and Chipper,' he replied, scratching the Doberman behind the ear.

'What are you doing here?' asked Aridain.

'The same as you, I'm here to find magical creatures.'

'They're so much fun to be with. Their words are always funny, talking about the weather, the trees, the frogs and the rabbits. They never stop chattering.'

'Is that right?' smiled Kale, squatting next to him. 'So how do you talk back, Aridain?'

'Can't you ask them?'

'I'm afraid not. They won't talk to me. I try but it's no use, perhaps they don't like me.'

Aridain remained silent for a moment, then turned back to Kale. 'They say they don't trust grown-ups, they say grown-ups' words are too serious and they don't understand.'

'That's alright, Aridain. I don't know any other grown-up who can talk to them either. Actually, while I'm here, I wanted to ask you…'

Kale suddenly looked around in confusion, his question eluding him like smoke through grasping fingers.

He looked down to see Aridain gazing at him expectantly. 'That's strange, my question seems to have completely slipped my mind.'

'You were going to ask me something about my friends.'

'No, that's not it… oh, I know, I wanted to ask you if…'

Again, Kale's thoughts drifted away like willow seeds on the breeze as he struggled to focus on what he was saying.

'Come on, Chipper, let's play. You can be Zakan The Wicked,' said Aridain abruptly. 'Do you want to play, Mr Kale? Uncle Keegan bought me a shield for my birthday, it's to go with my sword.'

As soon as Aridain left his side and picked up his sword, his mind immediately refocused and clarity hit him like a bolt from the blue. Catching up with the young tornado as he ran beside Chipper, with his sword flailing back and forth, Kale asked, 'So how old are you, Aridain?'

'Six,' he said proudly.

'Zakan The Wicked, huh? In my home village, we used to call him Zakan the Deceiver.'

'Why's that?' asked Aridain, suddenly intrigued.

'Many years ago, leading his evil horde and unable to break the school's defences, Zakan enchanted one of

Pellagrin's wizards, who showed him and his army into the school through a secret passage.'

Staring up at him with large, inquisitive hazel eyes, Aridain asked, 'What happened?'

'He was discovered, and just in time too.'

Now with clarity of mind Kale recognised what had thrown him from his train of thought so easily. *Too easily,* he admonished himself. Now that he had found it, he could feel the swirling magic of a spell surrounding this inquisitive young boy. But who had put it there, and what was it protecting?

'Mummy, Mummy look, this is my new friend, Kale,' shouted Aridain, running excitedly towards her.

Kale, I only know of one Kale, and he's a teacher at the school, thought Lascana suspiciously.

'He's a teacher at the school,' confirmed Aridain proudly.

'Really,' said Lascana, shutting the door to the cottage and watching as a figure, dressed in plain light and dark grey trousers, bodice and thick cloak, approached up the garden path. The man pulled back his hood, revealing friendly dark green eyes and a mass of light brown wavy hair. At Torsk's funeral she remembered Mace pointing out the good-looking young man who was to replace the vastly experienced wizard. At the time she had wondered how a young man, hardly any older than the students he taught, would cope with taking on the mantle of teacher tutoring creature lore.

'Mrs Bruin, hello,' he said in a friendly manner. 'I'm Kale, Torsk's replace…'

'I saw you at Torsk's funeral; unfortunately, I didn't get the chance to speak with you,' she said, instantly regretting the bluntness of her statement. 'I was sorry to hear of Torsk's untimely demise; he was a good, kindly man.'

Kale inclined his head and chuckled ironically. 'Since his death I realise how eminent a man he really was. His absence is an irreplaceable loss to the school and to me.'

'To all of us. So, what can I do for you, Mr Kale?' she inquired less assertively.

'He wants to ask me some very important questions, Mummy.'

'Actually, Aridain, before I do, I'd like to talk with your mother first, if that's all right?'

Not taking her eyes from Kale, Lascana ordered, 'Go and play in the garden with your new toys, Aridain, there's a good boy.'

'But, Mum…'

'Go now and play, and stay in the garden where I can see you!'

'Oh, alright,' said Aridain sulkily. 'What's the point of having a new friend if I can't play with him?'

Kale stared back at her through the eyes of a man who she guessed had been forced to grow up rapidly over the past couple of months.

'He certainly is an exceptional boy.'

'He's a handful, if that's what you mean.'

'Please, I mean no disrespect, and I don't mean to intrude,' he faltered. 'There's no easy way to put this, so I'll come straight to the point. I've witnessed Aridain's latent ability.'

'Excuse me?'

'I've seen what he can do.'

'Do?'

'Mrs Bruin, this is important.' Kale smiled a warm and genuine smile. 'I only want to help.'

Suddenly feeling as though she was about to be sick, Lascana, with tears in her eyes, looked despairingly at him. She swallowed quickly. 'I see.'

'It's difficult, I know.'

'What are you going to do?' she despaired.

'Do?' he exclaimed.

'Yes, now you've discovered the truth.'

'I don't understand?'

Uncertain how to respond, she smiled weakly. 'You had best come in so we can talk.' She led the way into the cottage's interior. 'Cup of tea?'

'Yes, please.'

After making the tea, Lascana led him into the dining room and, sitting opposite, placed his cup before him. She then looked at him at a loss, uncertain how to proceed.

'How did you find out?'

'I heard him talking with the woodland sprites in your garden.'

'Talking with woodland sprites?' she replied incredulously.

'Yes, you don't know?'

'No, I mean we knew he had an affinity with animals but...' she stopped suddenly. 'You're never really prepared, are you? We've been dreading this moment ever since he was born; it's something we've tried so hard to conceal over the years. We hoped his abilities would come to the fore after he attended school like other students, under the teachers' guidance. Only yesterday we discovered he can read minds. So, will you inform the school?' asked Lascana frostily.

'What? No, you misunderstand me.'

'Then what?'

'There's a Dark Creature roaming the grounds, and I wondered if you'd seen it? It ranges far afield and is returning regularly here, to the woods. I've been tasked to find it.'

Lascana looked at Kale warily. 'Creature?'

She was suddenly caught off guard as Kale asked, 'Tell me, was it Vara who cast the deflection spell?'

'Deflection spell?'

'Yes, someone cast the spell over your son. I'm surmising it was to distract anyone who might take advantage of him or his powers.'

'I was unaware of any spell casting concerning my son,' said Lascana ominously, her voice rising with every syllable. 'You're saying Vara cast a spell over my son, WITHOUT MY PERMISSION?'

'Well, she is a witch and Aridain's grandmother. Who else could it be?' said Kale hesitantly. 'Ah, she didn't tell you; well, don't worry Mrs Bruin it won't cause any problems. In fact, you should be thankful, as it may have saved your son's life without his knowledge.'

'Or without mine,' she fumed. 'She should have asked first. Can you tell when it was cast?'

'Don't blame yourself. You wouldn't have known unless you were with her at the time. It was more than likely at birth, it's the best time, and then after that the spell would have required a regular infusion to reinforce the magic, usually in the form of a potion-infused drink or food. It was a very good one too, nearly threw me off, but once I latched on to it, I realised it was hiding something. It grows with the individual, you see, so it's harder to...'

'You say a regular infusion; in the form of food or drink?' The penny suddenly dropped - 'Vara is always willing to take him off my hands when I'm busy and even provided a home for us when we needed it, it was the perfect opportunity to add an infusion to his food or drink.'

Walking to the dining room, Lascana took a deep breath and approaching the window looked outside, staring unseeingly into the mist shrouded garden. 'Aridain treats danger like some kind of game, you see, and like his father he has no fear, it seems.' Then suddenly she said, 'You think this creature is attracted to my son, don't you?'

'I can't be sure, not yet.'

'Don't treat me like a child, Kale. Vara reassured Alfic and me that his abilities were nothing special, that they held no significance!' She slowly turned from the window and looked at the young man sat opposite her, listening intently to her story, whom she had known for all of half an hour and with whom she now felt a strange affinity.

Smiling genuinely, he said, 'With your permission, I'd like to find out what your mother-in-law's spell is concealing?'

'If it will ascertain the truth....' considered Lascana. Then she looked towards the kitchen door. 'Aridain, I know you're there.'

Kale smiled as Aridain poked his head around the doorframe.

'Come over here, Dear and sit down,' said Lascana, shaking her head exasperatedly and pouring him a glass of milk.

'Something amusing?' asked Lascana.

'Oh sorry,' Kale chuckled. 'Just remembering the years of struggle, I have endured to attain my present rank as teacher, whereas Aridain, in his ignorance, seems to attract creatures as a matter of course.'

Lascana looked sideways at her son, who sat swinging his legs, a young boy who she now saw in a fresh light.

'Aridain, I'm going to press my palm against your forehead, it's a game we play at the school all the time,' instructed Kale. 'All I'm doing is looking inside your head; it's like hide and seek, the procedure is harmless. If you look hard enough, you will be able to see me too.'

'OK,' smiled Aridain, intrigued.

'Are you ready?'

Kale closed his eyes and pressed his palm gently to Aridain's forehead. At first, he could detect nothing unusual, so he pushed slightly harder. At first, there was resistance. Then abruptly the barrier eased, and he found himself falling into a vast expanse where a kaleidoscope of unlimited power and potential was laid bare. Unrestrained thoughts and emotions stretched out before him, dancing and weaving, dividing and re-forming. He found himself floating in a sea of unlimited imagination and grew giddy in the vast scope of possibilities spiralling and pirouetting before him.

He also sensed another presence, individual and separate from the boy's primeval mind. Like a distant beacon in the storm, it led him to the memory of Aridain's encounter with the creature. There was an all-pervading sense of approval as he watched, but as hard as he tried to grasp the entity, it remained elusive and untouchable. In time, a distant alien sound intruded into this astounding world and he swatted at it like an unwanted fly buzzing around his head, but the sound only became more insistent. Comprehension dawned on him as he recognised a young boy's shrill voice and, more distant still, a woman's insistent calls accompanied by the barking of a dog? A sudden jolt snapped him backwards and, with his head spinning, he grasped at the arms, which shook him roughly. Desperately holding on, he looked around in confusion and, feeling a small hand on his, turned and looked into the hazel eyes of a young, innocent boy.

'Aridain, I'm sorry, did I hurt you?' asked a concerned Kale as he held on tightly to Lascana's arms, the room still pirouetting around his head.

'A little,' said Aridain sadly, and then, more upbeat, 'you nearly fell off your chair. I know I'm six, but even you are too heavy for me.'

'We had to wake you,' smiled Lascana. 'My son said you were lost and couldn't find your way back.'

'Thank you, both,' he said, gingerly releasing Lascana's arm and wiping at the sweat dripping into his eyes.

'Can you come and play with me now?' Aridain said cheerfully, the fateful encounter seemingly not having affected him at all.

'I'll come and play with you shortly, I promise, but first I need to talk to your mother.'

Waiting until Aridain had left, Kale said, 'Mrs Bruin, do you know what kind of power your son has?'

'No, please, tell me.'

'I've been inside a few minds now, only to ascertain students' potential, you understand, but what I saw in Aridain astounded me. His potential, strength and sheer power dwarfed mine and all the evidence suggests that is what drew the Dark Creature here. Mrs Bruin, I was shown a vision of Perak and Aridain's encounter with the creature in the woods.'

Looking at Kale uncertainly, Lascana confirmed disconsolately, 'Yes, Perak said that it left a decaying dark rot in its wake. He also said this creature looked like Aridain; that it called him "Grandfather" and reached out for him. That was when Aridain and the Dark Creature touched; then there was a loud retort and a flash! Perak said it threw him and Aridain into the stream. What's going on Kale, do you know what this thing is?'

'He's in no danger yet, and I felt it couldn't hurt Aridain, but there's more. They're two halves of a whole, but unlike oil and water, the two can mix. And there's a need, a hunger that Aridain is not yet aware of, a hunger buried deep down inside.'

'So, what can we do about it?' she cried. 'He's just a boy.'

'I fear Aridain hasn't the luxury of time. It's imperative we find out why this doppelganger has appeared and what is its purpose. Your mother-in-law's deflection spell is good but, as Aridain grows up and his gift begins to blossom, he'll need other safeguards. I suggest that, instead of hiding Aridain's power, we need to help him develop it; it's going to be his only protection in the future. To be blunt, Mrs Bruin, if I can see past this spell then so could others, and if the "wrong sort" picks up on his magic… If we don't do something promptly, Aridain's "talent" will be too great to stop or control; he needs teaching.'

Tears welled up in Lascana's eyes, but she turned to Kale determined, nonetheless. 'No one is taking my son,' she growled. 'I WON'T ALLOW IT.' Then more gently, 'Can you teach him?'

'Don't look at me. I suggest your sister-in-law, Magen; she would be the obvious choice. There's one more thing, a disturbing thing. This may sound strange, but I think he has a resident up here,' said Kale, pointing to his head.

'What do you mean?' exclaimed Lascana.

'I think he has a companion.'

'How do you know this?'

'It led me to the memory.'

'Oh, and that makes it all right then?' said Lascana. 'Kale, don't we have to get it out? This entity may prove harmful! Do you know who or what it is? Is this normal?'

'I couldn't get near enough and, no, it certainly isn't normal, but I sensed only benevolence.'

Lascana threw her hands in the air in exasperation. 'Even so, it's just one more thing to worry about. I'm sorry; I shouldn't take my frustrations out on you. Thank you for caring, Kale, although I don't know why you should. After all, we've only just met!'

Kale smiled. 'Aridain reminds me of my dilemma as a youth and your fortitude reminds me of my mother.'

'Really?'

'Really,' Kale nodded, then smiled. 'Now, I have a promise to fulfil.'

As he stood up to go and play with Aridain, Lascana cleared her throat and grasped Kale's hands in hers. 'When you've finished playing, I want you to tell me all you know. I need all the information you have so that I can protect my son.'

Kale smiled and nodded. 'Very well, Mrs Bruin.'

'Good, then I'll put the kettle on while you go and play with Aridain, and please call me Lascana.'

The grey afternoon had lengthened into a glorious evening as Alfic, a brace of rabbits in hand, made his way back to the cottage, the setting sun turning the underside of the cloud layer a glorious deep shade of purple. Whistling a cheerful tune, a sharp pain in his rear soon jolted him back to reality, and swinging his empty lunch bag around his head, he bolted up the incline to his home with a cluster of angry hornet flies in hot pursuit. It was only when he reached his front door that the persistent insects finally gave up. However, upon opening the door, he found his pain had only just begun.

'Daddy,' screamed Aridain, launching himself towards Alfic and wrapping himself around his leg.

'Hello, Munchkin,' he gasped from between clenched teeth. 'Don't squeeze so hard.'

'Hello, husband of mine,' shouted Lascana. 'I thought you were lambing.'

Rubbing vigorously at his backside, which throbbed painfully, Alfic replied, 'All of a sudden, the younger hands have volunteered... I wonder why?' said Alfic sardonically, rolling his eyes.

'Ahh, the school fair,' proclaimed Lascana, reaching up and kissing him on the cheek.

'Uh huh,' agreed Alfic, rubbing his thumbs and forefingers together. 'They want to earn more money.'

'They're young men. They won't miss a chance to use it to entice the girls from the surrounding villages,' she offered. 'What's wrong?'

'Flaming hornet flies stung me again. After tea, I'm going down there to destroy that confounded nest,' hissed Alfic, rubbing at his backside.

'Do you want me to rub it better?' winked Lascana.

'Mummy, that's horrible. Why would you want to rub Daddy's bottom?' exclaimed Aridain, making a face.

'One day you'll understand, dear,' smiled Lascana.

'Come on, Chipper, let's go back into the garden,' shouted Aridain.

'Oh no you don't, it's wash time for you, young man. After playing in the garden all day, you smell like a warthog.'

'Oh, Muuum.'

'Go on, off you go, the water's already poured, put your dirty clothes in the wash basket, I'll be in to check on you later.'

As Aridain slouched away, Alfic followed Lascana into the kitchen, sniffing the air eagerly. 'Hmmm, smells delicious, and I'm famished,' he said, smiling at Lascana half-heartedly.

'Here, smear this on. Vara swears by it, it's a salve made from Pennyroyal, Dock and Beechnut.'

After applying the salve, Alfic retreated to the small, cosy living room with its wooden ceiling beams and whitewashed walls hung with pictures and ornamental plates that Lascana had collected over the years. He stared through the lead cut glass of Lascana's ornament cabinet displaying her collection of artefacts, glittering in the firelight's flickering flames. It was ironic that, with everything they disagreed on, collecting rare and strange artefacts was one of the few things Lascana had in common with his mother. *It was just a pity they couldn't agree on anything else* he thought ironically.

Later that evening, having tucked in Aridain for the night, Alfic sat thoughtfully in front of the fire repairing a straw basket, while Lascana sat humming contentedly as she darned a pair of Aridain's socks. After talking to Lascana it seemed that not only had his own mother been performing spells on their son but also, according to Kale, this creature was attracted to a power that Vara had dismissed as normal- although according to Kale it seemed anything but; the result of the encounter between Aridain and the creature having caused the school to commission the young Animistic to investigate. He also knew for a fact that his mother often had her own agenda and put her own selfish needs above all else. Rubbing Chipper behind the ears, he leant forward and stoked the fire, then shook his head angrily, thinking, *why do all the problems always lead back to Mother? After all these years, she's still an enigma wrapped up in secrecy!*

He ran his hands through his thick black mane of hair, then turned his thoughts to the creature teacher, Kale. Lascana said that he was genuinely concerned about Aridain but, instead of taking on the job himself, he had recommended Magen to instruct Aridain in the ways of magic. He had also found out that, like himself, Kale had suspicions over Torsk's death. Could he be trusted? That remained to be seen. 'Where my son is concerned, I'm taking no chances and if anyone threatens him, they will answer to me,' he hissed under his breath.

'What's that, dear?'

'Nothing; just thinking aloud.'

A pop brought him back to reality and before his eyes a smoking ember arched lazily through the air and landed in the silken fabric of Lascana's favourite rug. Picking it up and juggling it between his fingers, he threw the hot piece of wood back into the fire before it could burn a hole in the Argol sheep and reedmace moth thread.

'Aridain's fast asleep, Chipper,' said Alfic. 'Want to help me kill off those damn hornets?'

Canting his head sideways and raising his droopy ears, Chipper, looking intently at Alfic, wagged his tail.

'That's settled then; come on, let's go.'

'Be careful, that thing is out there somewhere,' stressed Lascana.

Kissing Lascana soundly, he said confidently, 'I'll be fine.'

Having grabbed his axe, Alfic, with Chipper trotting contentedly at his side, walked hastily down the garden path, holding the lamp nervously out in front despite his bravado and peering into the night.

'OK, boy, from now on we have to be cautious.'

Chipper issued a small yap that Alfic took to mean that he understood. They took the path into the wood and climbed through the thick bramble hedge that covered the bank next to the bridge. Setting the lamp down in between the twisted roots of a gnarly black poplar, he then waded into the stream with axe in hand while Chipper sat quietly watching from the bank. Creeping as quietly as he could into the middle of the fast-flowing stream, swollen with the recent thaw, he ducked beneath the underside of the bridge, quite prepared to wade in up to his neck, if necessary, to destroy the nest and its troublesome inhabitants. Feeling the water's chill seeping through his clothes, the oil lamp softy illuminating the melon-sized nest humming softly above his head, he gripped the axe in both hands and, taking a deep breath, swung at the cord holding the nest, severing it cleanly. Then, before the hornets could swarm, he quickly pushed it beneath the water, planting his foot firmly on top until he drowned the colony. With a self-satisfied grunt Alfic announced, 'Sting me, will you, you cursed insects!' Wading back to the bank, he climbed out and, taking Chipper's head in his hands, rubbed his ears affectionately. 'They won't be bothering us anymore, eh, boy?'

He looked up sharply as Chipper tensed and then growled. Almost immediately, an unearthly cry followed that echoed through the night.

'What in Inver's teeth was that?' hissed Alfic apprehensively. Grasping the lamp in one hand and the axe in the other, he peered into the darkness. 'It wasn't a fox, that's for sure. Come on, boy, let's take a look.'

Gripping the axe tighter still and resisting the urge to run, Alfic swung the lamp back and forth as he walked cautiously into the gloom. His breath coming in short gasps, he swallowed hard as something moved against the darkness and Chipper, growling ominously, pranced frantically back and forth. Suddenly a shard of night in the shape of a small child detached itself from the surrounding darkness with sinewy outstretched arms; it was the Dark Creature. On closer inspection Alfic realised its resemblance to Aridain was only transitory and, struggling to keep his fear in check, raised his axe to strike.

'What are you and what do you want with my family?'

'Faaarrtthhherrr,' said the figure awkwardly, peering at him with small, yellow, beady eyes. 'Kin-dr-ed, fa-mi-ly,' it stuttered.

'Father! What do you mean, "father"? How could I give life to something like you? You're not even human,' said Alfic angrily. Then, with more conviction, he said, 'Find another family, you can't have mine.'

It then opened its mouth and a nightmarish call, akin to a distressed cat, pierced the night, sending chills down Alfic's spine and causing Chipper to whimper and recoil in fear. The creature suddenly lunged at him with extended arms and Alfic, casting the lamp aside, swung his axe, the blade cleaving the Dark Creature like a knife into butter. The creature looked unconcernedly at the axe embedded between its head and shoulder, then peered up at him with pitiful yellow eyes.

'You should not have done that fa-ther,' said the Dark Creature in a nightmarish voice. 'Now I mu-ssst kill you.'

Trying to wrench the axe from its body, Alfic suddenly looked down in horror as blackness enveloped the axe head, which then began creeping up the handle towards him. Alfic quickly snatched his hand away as the creature, looking so forlorn and helpless a few moments previously, suddenly took on the demeanour of an enraged harpy. As the yellow eyes advanced towards him through the darkness, Alfic backed away and, stumbling over a root, tumbled down the bank into the swollen stream. Coughing and spluttering, Alfic surfaced and braced his body against the fast-flowing water. He peered anxiously into the darkness and watched as Chipper, with a snarl, ran and sunk his sharp teeth into the Dark Child's flank. However, the creature seemed totally unconcerned. The creature then watched, as if spellbound, as the Doberman ceased its attack, retreated and stood listlessly licking at froth-caked jaws.

'Chipper?' questioned Alfic, wading towards the bank. 'What's wrong, boy? Come here.'

The Doberman turned and, with menacing yellow and black-streaked eyes, glared at him like a hound born of a nightmare. With sharp incisor teeth bared in a feral grimace, more akin to a rabid Ardent Wolf than a loving pet, the Doberman snarled in warning, causing Alfic to stumble back involuntarily into the fast-flowing water once more. He stared at their family pet, now a shell purged of loyalty and faithfulness; possessed by the Dark Creature's otherworldly malice. With slavering jaws bared, snapping teeth and claws slashing, it leapt from the bank, landing in a cascade of water in the midst of the fast-flowing current. Reaching down into the water, Alfic grasped a fist-sized rock from the streambed and with strength born of desperation; he threw the stone at their family pet.

Unaffected, the Doberman kept coming so, locating more rocks on the streambed, Alfic struck out again and again. Regardless of the heavy blows, the Doberman, now crazed with rage, thrashed towards him: its jaw splintered, its teeth shattered, its face a mess of blood and bone. He watched the crazed Doberman, now blind and bloodied, swimming in aimless circles in an effort to locate him. Breathing heavily from his exertions, Alfic waded through the water and with tears of anger and despair he pummelled at the dog, now certain in the knowledge that if it bit him, he too would become an unwilling servant of this agent of evil.

'I'm sorry, Chipper.'

Seizing the animal firmly by its neck and back, he thrust it below the water; surely it must die without air. In an effort to reach the surface, the Doberman squirmed and thrashed but, resolutely, Alfic held the dog down, feeling its struggles slowly cease until it remained still. Wiping angrily at the tears streaming down his face, Alfic looked up at the Dark Creature, staring back at him expressionlessly.

'So, what are you waiting for? You've killed my dog; now come and finish me. Come on, kill me.'

The creature stood glancing quickly, first at him and then to the water for what seemed an age. Then, with a mournful howl, it turned and left Alfic in the dark.

His nerves jangling, he retrieved the Doberman from underfoot and, hoisting Chipper's soaked, bloodstained corpse over his shoulder, he climbed up the bank. Reasonably assured that the Dark Creature had gone, he looked down forlornly at the battered corpse laying on the bank, now free of the creature's infection, and gently stroked his fur. 'How am I going to explain this to my son, he'll never understand?'

After what seemed like an age, he hoisted the limp body over his shoulder and headed disconsolately for home.

That same night Kuelack sat in his apartment together with Ramus as they studied worn and faded manuscripts piled upon the top of his thick wooden desk. Looking up irritably as the bell above his head jangled noisily, he smiled, commanding the entrance door to open with a thought. 'Come in, gentlemen.'

'Master Ramus,' bowed Tallus respectfully entering the candle lit office.

Kuelack, with Ramus stood serenely at his side, nodded to the tall, lithe figure of Tallus as he glided silently into the room dressed in the long white and brown edged cloak of Animistic apprentice, his hawk-like face set in an odious grimace as with deep, dark, opal eyes he studied his surroundings. It was a grimace that Kuelack knew stemmed from the discomfort he felt at having to wear the uniform of a student rather than a Master of his art; it was an oversight soon to be addressed. In his wake scuttled the furtive, enigmatic figure of Mass Martin, dressed in the white and plain green-bordered attire of Master Psychic. The two men looked worlds apart. Tallus, the apprentice, exuded power and a ruthless demeanour, while the master of minds who had few friends due to his mind reading abilities, appeared weary, cautious and hesitant. Focusing on Ramus at his back, he realised that Tallus and Mass weren't the only pair as different as chalk and cheese.

Gliding across his private office, Kuelack noticed that Tallus was standing imperiously at the window, looking out on to the darkened courtyard, hands clasped behind his back, while Mass sat quietly with his eyes closed and his fingers pressed together in front of his face.

Spinning around to face them, Tallus asked in his deep, rasping voice, 'How is Gradine, Master? Good, I trust.'

'She is well.'

'And did you enjoy my performance at the assembly?' smiled Mass. 'Almagest and Magen left none the wiser, as I promised.'

'Let's hope it stays that way, for your sake,' warned Ramus disdainfully.

'Gentlemen, it's time you were appraised of the next step of my plan.'

'About time,' declared Mass.

Kuelack shot Mass a warning glance. 'As I was just explaining to Ramus here, I have been seeking the whereabouts of the Firebrand stone thanks to a certain diary I unearthed,' he said tetchily.

'The Firebrand stone?' questioned Mass, smiling confidently. 'Pellagrin and his followers destroyed that cursed artefact.'

'It was a lie. The stone was only split into four equal segments and hidden in secret places all over Aymara.'

'But, master, if this is true...'

'It means that, with the shards in my possession, nothing can stop us.'

'How long will this search take? How will you find them?' queried Mass.

'It is none of your concern, but until we return, you must move cautiously and quietly. If anyone asks, Ramus and I are away on official business.'

'And if Almagest, Exedra, or your sister ask where you are?' asked Mass sceptically. 'If they suspect what we're doing, they will attempt to stop us before we are ready.'

'The fight has left my sister, she will do nothing; Almagest, on the other hand, will be called away on a fool's errand,' sneered Kuelack.

Pouring himself a glass of Navarian brandy and savouring its deep oak fermented fire, he suddenly turned towards them; Kuelack knew that the dark wizards of old would have been less than pleased with Mass's blasé attitude. Moreover, judging from Tallus and especially Ramus's disapproving stares towards the bald psychic and seeing their reservations and questions mirrored there, it confirmed their discontent.

'Kuelack. What about your brother, Alfic? If he discovers what we are planning, it's certain he will intervene,' said Ramus, 'and where he leads, his friends will follow.'

'These individuals pose no real threat,' said Mass dismissively.

'I agree, the gardener's glory days are over,' said Tallus.

'This may be true, but we must still proceed with caution until the time is right. Stick to the plan for now, our time will come soon enough. If we move against the wrong people too soon, it will only rally support for them, and if my brother decides to intervene, I'll deal with him,' he said vehemently.

'What about Exedra, Master, surely she's a threat?'

'She is of no concern, Tallus,' said Kuelack matter-of-factly, turning menacingly toward Mass Martin, who was chuckling excitedly, his head bobbing around like an agitated owl.

'I have altered the lightning mistress's perceptions. A powerful sorceress she may be, but her mental perception leaves a lot to be desired,' chuckled Mass confidently.

'Hence the very reason we voted her on to the council in the first place,' continued Kuelack irritably. 'I presume, Mass, that your progress with Exedra is on schedule?'

'Of course, and might I say…'

'You may not!'

Turning towards the disconsolate young Tallus, Kuelack said, 'Tallus; you think that my recommending your class tutor Kale Simm to investigate this creature was a mistake.'

'He is a talent-less fool, Master.'

'So I thought. I appointed him thinking his naivety, his lack of experience, would cause him to fail and gain us some time,' said Kuelack irritably. 'However, I have underestimated the Pheton born youngster, which is why it's time for you, Tallus, to prove yourself. Search out the truth and report back to me with your findings.'

'I'm looking forward to contributing to the cause. It's about time a real Animistic looked into this problem. Also, contact Hogan, and tell him to report to me. I have need of his skills.'

'As you wish, Master.'

'That is all,' said Kuelack abruptly.

Ramus turned to Kuelack. 'I don't trust him or his ability to creep around inside people's heads,' hissed

Ramus, watching Mass Martin as he followed Tallus out of the door. 'Mind Masters are a law unto themselves: neither Dark magic nor Light.'

'Like it or not, for now we need this one.' Then, tidying the papers on his desk, Kuelack continued, 'Don't fret Dragon Lord, Mass's time will come, as will that of all who oppose me.'

Voices, followed by the sound of footsteps, echoed along the corridor and Magen, with heart pounding, turned from her position beside Kuelack's door. Retreating to her own apartment, she uttered a nervous whispered word and with a wave of her hand the lock to her apartment clicked opened and she slipped inside.

Her thoughts spinning from the conversation she had just overheard, she closed the door behind her and with her back pressed against it, shook her head in consternation.

The Firebrand stone; deliberately voting Exedra on to the council; sending Almagest on a fool's errand. It all beggared belief! The strange conversation with Kuelack in the Assembly Hall should have triggered alarm bells. I should have seen this, she thought. *Kuelack, who despised weakness, had always been competitive and ambitious since his schooldays; having chosen the Dark over the Light.* She shook her head in dismay. *All this time pretending, pretending to be something he's not.*

A small voice jolted her from these thoughts. 'Mummy, is that you?'

'Hello little one, what are you doing out of bed?'

'You're late again. I missed you Mummy,' she said, stumbling sleepily into Magen's arms.

Two years older than her cousin Aridain, Ferula had dark hair tied in pigtails that trailed down her back and a face full of freckles (inherited from her father, Beaty).

'Where's Linden? He's supposed to be looking after you.'

'I'm in here, Mother.'

Linden, two years older than Ferula, was sitting intently in front of a canvas painting of the school in his room. He had the same tanned features and fine, light coloured hair as Aridain, and people often thought mistakenly that they were brothers.

'I told you Mother would be home soon, Ferula; when Father's away I'm the man of the house,' he said proudly.

'And a fine job you do. Have you eaten?' asked Megan.

'Of course,' declared Linden indignantly.

'Then you should be in bed,' she said, ushering them back into the dining room.

'Five minutes, Mother, then I'll be finished.'

'How are the studies coming along, Linden?'

'Ok, Teacher Merle said I'll be able to translocate simple items soon, although I'm having difficulty refining complicated pictures.'

'I'm sure you'll do fine, dear,' she said, kissing his hair. 'You feel cold,' she said, kneeling next to him and feeling his hand.

'I've been painting.'

'But I'm toasty warm,' smiled Ferula.

'I've never heard of a handshaking as the result of intense painting.'

'Don't worry, Mother, it's not just painting, my teacher said it's the result of too much practise.'

'Then don't practise quite so hard,' said Magen impatiently while glancing anxiously towards the door she feared would open to reveal her angry brother at any time.

'I can identify all the different Rorqual birds in Srinigar,' said Ferula sleepily.

'Yes, I'm sure you can, dear. Now hurry back to bed. I've things to do,' she said irritably.

'Who cares about Rorqual birds?' quipped Linden.

'Yes, yes; now hurry up, to bed, NOW,' she shouted, instantly regretting her harsh tone.

'Mother, are you alright?'

'Yes, I'm fine, Linden.' She took a deep, calming breath. 'I just have a lot on my mind.' She gave them both a big hug. 'Now; off to bed, both of you.'

She watched as they closed the doors to their rooms and then began tidying the dining room into some semblance of order. Squaring her shoulders, she came to a decision; in the morning, she would confront her brother.

CHAPTER SIX

REVELATIONS

'Aridain, stop crying now,' said Lascana, gently crouching before Aridain. 'Aridain, look at me,' she said more insistently.

It was the next morning and Aridain sat at the table with his head buried in his folded arms, looked up at her with tear-filled eyes.

'It wasn't anyone's fault. The creature tried to kill your father and Chipper tried to protect him just as he protected you so many times before.'

'But Mummy, why didn't Daddy do something?'

'This thing, whatever it is, was too strong, too dangerous.'

'If I was there, I'd have saved Chipper.' He began to cry again.

'Nobody wants to kill, Aridain, and nobody wants to die, but sometimes those choices are taken away from us.'

'It's done,' called a morose Alfic from the hallway.

Lascana looked at him harshly as he entered the kitchen and shook her head.

'Mummy, I know what Daddy is talking about.'

She watched sadly as Alfic knelt down in front of Aridain, took his small hands in his and said helplessly,

'I'm sorry, Munchkin, there was nothing I could do. At least in the grove the evil will never infect him again.'

'Perhaps my friends will look after him, make him better,' exclaimed Aridain brightly.

'Aridain, nothing can bring him back.' Alfic looked up at Lascana who nodded, then said, 'Say, why don't I...'

'I DON'T WANT ANOTHER DOG, I WANT CHIPPER BACK,' shouted Aridain, and he ran from the room.

'Telepathy?' stated Alfic.

'Telepathy,' confirmed Lascana. 'I told you Kale said his mind was extraordinary.' She looked sympathetically into her husband's eyes. 'He'll be alright; he just needs time. This wasn't your fault, so don't blame yourself.'

'I was the one who encouraged Chipper to follow me into the night; I was the one who battered our dog to a bloody pulp with a rock. How can I tell him that? He'll never understand; he'll hate me!'

'Alfic, you said so yourself. Chipper was under the control of that "Thing"; there was no doubt.'

'Chipper wasn't just a pet; he was a loyal friend, part of this family.'

Lascana watched her husband as he slumped down heavily in a chair, his eyes growing distant as the full tumult of last night's events played out once more across his vision.

'What does this thing want?' he cried. 'It called me "Father", Lascana, why?'

'Its face is the exact likeness of Aridain. What if it was conceived at the same time? Perak said it looked at him longingly as it did you; it seems to think we're its family.'

'Being created in our son's image - to thinking we're its family is a giant leap of conjecture, Lascana.'

'Well, we have to do something, dear husband of mine, because until we do... this thing will continue to stalk us.'

'Yes, you're right, of course. But what? I'll have a word with Mother.'

'And I'll make enquiries at work,' said Lascana, 'which reminds me; it's time I opened the store.'

Having tried and failed to eat even a morsel of breakfast served in the main food hall, Magen walked apprehensively up the grand stairwell of the Administration wing; pass the Fighting Masters' and teachers' floors to the third floor. Turning right down the lavender infused corridor, her footsteps echoing from the dimly lit walls and ceiling, she passed the thick oak doors to the Wizard's quarters with their privileged views across the school grounds and the surrounding fields. Pausing, she looked up at the portrait of Sorceress Cardia, one of many portraits hung along the walls and in between each apartment, her familiar steely countenance and serene blue eyes smiling down at her confidently. Cardia was a woman she had greatly admired, and her untimely death had come as a shock to everyone and especially to her. She missed Cardia's calming words of wisdom and reassuring presence on the high council. No doubt the stalwart sorceress would have known what to do in this situation, whereas she positively loathed the confrontation to come.

Yawning, as much from trepidation as tiredness, she continued towards the end of the corridor where her rooms and the more prestigious lodgings reserved for the Sivan council were located. She then stopped and turned as the door she had just passed opened inwards. From out of the shimmering, deep red interior a tall, imposing figure appeared and stared down at her from red, fiery eyes.

'Ramus?'

She rarely ever saw the Dragon Lord off duty, so it was a shock to see him dressed not in the plain white and red dragon's head adorned robes of a teacher, but in a pair of dark shimmering baggy pants and a red open-sleeved shirt. Far from softening his hard external façade, his matching head of dark hair, neatly cropped moustache and beard made the Dragon Lord, from the volcanic desolation of the Zapata highland plains, appear even more fearsome.

'Magen? Can I have a word?'

Ramus was a secretive individual; his art dictated they had little in common, so the invitation surprised her.

'Not right now, I've a meeting with…'

'No need to trouble Kuelack.' Then, fixing her with an intense stare, he insisted, 'It's important, it's about last night.'

'Very well,' she said guardedly.

'But not here, inside.'

Following him through to his living quarters in silence, Magen unclasped her pale green shawl and mopped her sweaty brow in the uncomfortable heat.

'You look terrible, sleepless night?'

Yawning again, Magen said, 'Yes, something like that, although I'm not surprised to see those who study dragon lore awake in the twilight hours.'

'Dragons and those who practise their lore don't need much sleep.'

Observing the dark lava-furnished, flame-lit room, the interior hadn't changed from her last visit. Flaming torches burned from mounts, set into the stonewalls, surrounding a magnificent black alabaster fireplace from where a multi-coloured fire burned, giving the room the appearance of a bejewelled cavern.

Flapping the lapels of her blouse in the heat of the room, she gazed at the skeleton of a firedrake, hanging menacingly from the ceiling. 'You're still collecting trophies, I see,' said Magen nervously.

'These "trophies" make the place feel more homely,' said Ramus, taking a long gulp of the dark liquid and revealing his set of sharp, gleaming white teeth. 'Reminds me of my home.' He took a square pewter pot from a tall brass tripod and poured a thick dark liquid into a cup that Magen knew wasn't coffee.

'Drink?' he said in his deep, booming, no-nonsense voice.

'No, thank you.'

Also adorning the shelves and tables, displayed like prized possessions were jars and bottles filled with pickled dragons' remains and the mummified carcasses of their smaller cousins, while on his desk, taking pride of place, was the razor-like skull of a dragonlet. However, the most prized object in the room, she knew, was his extremely rare dragon-scaled cloak, which stood in the corner draped over a tailor's wooden mannequin.

'They are magnificent, regal beasts, but I'm happy they were driven from our skies; they are dangerous creatures, to be sure,' commented Megan.

'So say all who live in ignorance,' countered Ramus. 'They are seriously misunderstood creatures, who wanted nothing but to be left alone.'

'You said, "who"?'

'Yes, they are individuals, not animals controlled by instinct; they feel and they mourn for members of their race. Man's greed and seizure of their lands is a travesty.'

'Surely you can't be serious, favouring these beasts above your own kind?'

'My own kind,' Ramus mused. 'Yes, I'm very serious. I pity man's fear and ignorance of the unknown.'

Angry now, and feeling completely out of her depth, Magen cleared her throat and growled, 'What do you want, Ramus? I have more important things to do than waste my time with idle banter.' She then took a pace backwards as Ramus drew himself to his full height and looked down at her contemptibly.

'Events will soon favour the bold and the bold get their rewards,' said Ramus, walking over to his desk. He then peered at her ambiguously while tenderly stroking the delicate, jagged skull of the dragonlet.

'Meaning?'

'Meaning; in the end, my art will compensate me handsomely for my diligence.'

'You said you had information concerning the meeting with my brother last night.'

'Meeting?' said Ramus abruptly. 'I said nothing about a meeting.'

Realising the trap, she'd fallen into and attempting to take the initiative, Magen said, 'I overheard the conversation, the one in Kuelack's rooms. You were there, don't deny it, Ramus.'

Ramus looked down at her with a disagreeable frown. 'Eavesdropping Magen is highly unethical.'

'Nonetheless Ramus, I overheard Kuelack say he's located one of the Firebrand shards. Tell me that I misheard?'

'You misheard. The Firebrand stone was destroyed, you know that as well as I,' said Ramus, changing tack and studying her face in turn.

Megan thought, *Famous wizards like Pellagrin, Sakar, Rueben and Devine previously occupied these very chambers; they had fought and overcome far greater challenges than this. What must their spirits be thinking of her, as she stood in trepidation before the imposing Dragon Master, incapable of backing her accusations with action?*

'I also overheard Mass boasting over his control of Exedra and say, "We must move quietly, for if Almagest, myself or Exedra suspect what we are doing, they will try to stop us,"' she said, 'these were Mass's very words, were they not?'

'They are of no concern; Exedra and Almagest are completely unaware.'

'Well, you should be concerned about Almagest's and Exedra's reaction once I tell them what you're planning.'

'Well, well, perhaps your brother was mistaken when he said the fight had left you.'

In the sudden uncomfortable silence Magen watched, attempting to gauge Ramus's mood as he walked slowly from his desk towards the back of the room.

'The other day, when Kuelack asked if I would fight to protect the school, I thought nothing of it at the time, but after last night, it all fits. My brother's planning some kind of takeover of the school with the help of you, Mass and Tallus, isn't he?' Buoyed by her intuition and Ramus's silence, she said, 'I also think Cardia discovered this plan and was killed for her trouble. Tell me my imagination isn't running away with me.'

'Very clever, Magen,' said Ramus, donning his cloak. 'I'm sorry you had to find out this way; you must understand this is nothing personal – you were just in the wrong place at the wrong time.'

'I am your superior, and I'm ordering you to tell me what's going on,' commanded Magen, now feeling very uncomfortable in the tense atmosphere.

'I'm truly sorry, but I can allow no one to ruin my plans.'

'Your plans? Don't you mean Kuelack's plans?' She glared at the silent Ramus.

'It's not too late, Magen. Join me. Together we could stop Kuelack and take the shards for ourselves.'

'I will not be party to murder and genocide,' cried Magen, shaking her head miserably.

'Then I'm sorry, you leave me no choice.'

Suddenly, Magen's world turned fiery red. Out of pure instinct she reacted, deflecting the intense flame that suddenly battered at her hastily erected defences. Sobbing in disbelief, her only thought was that of flight. Ramus's barrage of fire forced her backwards, threatening to breach her barrier, singeing her clothes and pinning her against the wall. Managing to gather her wits, Magen, with a power born of desperation, turned the fire back upon its source, the wall of flames hurling the unprepared Ramus backwards.

Rising to his feet, Ramus triumphed, 'Flames cannot harm me, I was born of this.'

With a wave of her hands, Magen burst open the door and then sent the deadly splinters spinning and scything towards Ramus.

Lacking the mettle for a confrontation, her courage having left her at the thought of having to fight, with smoke billowing from her garments she burst into the corridor with a sob, her first instinct to seek the safety of her apartment. Bewildered, she turned, but realising Ramus's imposing figure blocked the way. She forced her trembling legs to stand and then ran down the corridor. Reaching a particular door, she banged hard, 'Savarin, Savarin help, I need your help now!'

Behind her, Ramus shouted, 'Your mistimed heroics are too late, Magen, Almagest has left on a fool's errand and won't be returning... ever.' Then more calmly he said, 'Tell me, do you know what the half giant Hogan did before he worked at the school?'

Magen span around with her back pressed against the door and watched Ramus, full of confidence and passion, stride towards her. She looked down at her shaking hands and her scorched garments. 'No; leave me alone, I don't want to harm you.'

'Harm me?' sneered Ramus. 'The fight isn't in you, Magen, we both know that.'

Ramus was right, but the fight hadn't left her recently, the fight had left her years ago, her time on the council slowly dulling her senses, the result - apathy.

'He was an assassin, a bandit.'

'No,' she despaired.

'And Hogan is very good at what he does. Almagest will not return to the school. That is why you have to join with me. Together we can foil your brother's plans; bring order to the school.'

'No, I will not hear this. Almagest is one of the most pre-eminent mages in the land!' screamed Magen. 'I don't believe you.'

Suddenly she fell into the doorway as it opened and lay staring up at the dark countenance of Savarin, the school's master of all things connected to the weather.

Donning a thick sheep's wool robe, Savarin studied her smouldering clothes with dark brooding grey eyes from beneath straight black hair. Looking up at Ramus, he demanded, 'What is going on here? Magen, are you alright?' Stepping in front of Magen protectively, Savarin asked darkly, 'Mind telling me why Magen's robes are scorched, Ramus?'

Climbing to her feet, straightening what was left of her clothes and attempting to regain a modicum of her dignity, Magen stepped in between them and then turned to Savarin, 'It's alright, I'm fine, a minor disagreement, nothing more.' She then peered at Ramus markedly. 'And you're leaving, right, Ramus?'

'Trust me; this isn't over, Magen Breed.' Ramus then turned and glided toward his apartment.

As the carriage bounced along the rutted road, Almagest gazed out of the window across the hedgerows and rolling green chequerboard countryside, watching in fascination as hard-working villagers, bathed in late morning spring sunshine, scythed corridors through the fields of spring corn, while others collected and threw the tied sheaths up to men balanced upon horse draw wagons.

Despite the carriage's sumptuous ride, it had been a long and uncomfortable two days' journey along the rough shingle road, punctuated only by an uncomfortable night's sleep at the Islip Inn in the village of Pheton; in an effort to take his mind off of the bone jarring journey, he turned his thoughts to their next stop, the village of Bryony.

Bryony sat overlooking 'The Blinks', an escarpment that dropped suddenly 1500 feet to the Gondarian plain below. Renowned for its smooth clay, its clay works fashioned pots, pans and tableware, shipping its goods all over the realm. The works even made commissioned items for the royal court in Gonda.

The escarpment itself was a dangerous place, feared and respected by the people who decided to settle nearby. It was rumoured to retain a primitive awareness from the Wild Durbah of millennia past, a place that aggressively resisted any attempt to encroach upon or reduce its boundaries further. The undergrowth and vegetation constantly trying to reclaim the highway down through its midst, much to the annoyance of the authorities.

Closing his eyes, Almagest pondered Mace's and Kale's revelation that a strange creature was roaming the countryside. A creature that was killing both livestock and people but had so far killed none at the school, only men from the King's land adjacent to the school; could it be that the school's magic wasn't so dormant after all? Had Kuelack summoned this thing as a part of his increasingly aggressive stance? And why, as Kale had indicated, did the Dark Creature think that Perak's family was its own. When he returned, he would address these problems and many more. He would call for a vote to remove Kuelack from the council table. He shook his head and smiled; he was kidding himself. The confrontation, whatever form it took, would end in a fight. Kuelack, he knew, wouldn't be dictated to, while he himself was not prepared to relinquish control and leave the school in the hands of a power-hungry despot.

Could he count on the support of the other council members? For instance, would family ties bind Magen or would she support her school principal and do what was right for the school? And then there was Exedra's recent strange behaviour; it now seemed it also involved the Mind Master. Becoming concerned, though against his better judgement, he had had a quick foray through her mind and discovered Mass's mental fingerprint there. Was he working alone, or was Mass under orders to tamper with Exedra's mind? It was just one more piece to fit into the puzzle.

But he knew he couldn't do this alone. When he returned, he would approach the people who opposed Kuelack, people at the school he knew and could trust such as Perak and Alfic, Weather Master Savarin and

Rasbora (Mistress of the Elements). A jolt roused him from his deliberations, and he opened his eyes.

'The village of Bryony is just up ahead, Sir.'

'Good. How long to change the horses, Phipps? We can't delay.'

'Twenty minutes, Sir.'

'Good, I need to conclude my business in Gonda and get back to the school as soon as possible.'

Twenty minutes later and, true to his word, Phipps had changed horses and, munching on a hastily bought meat pie, had urged the fresh team of horses forward.

Having left the village of Bryony behind, the rhythmic pounding of the horses' hooves began to slow as the terrain began its inexorable climb towards The Blinks. To curb his growing frustration, Almagest studied the countryside, which had grown more sheer and rugged, and the farmland which, instead of open fields of freshly planted wheat and barley, was now dotted with herds of sheep and cattle. The construction material of the stone buildings had changed from light grey granite blocks to sandstone, and the vegetation was more condensed, the trees and plants clumping together as if trying to protect The Blinks and what was left of its former glory.

As they continued to climb, he became increasingly aware of vegetation from The Blinks such as sharp-spined Cleaver trees, the lethal Burdock Orchid and Rumble trees that moved when no one was looking in a never-ending search for more fertile soil, growing amongst the more benign plant life. By mid-afternoon the terrain had levelled off and they once again made good time towards the escarpment edge.

Before they descended into the trees, Almagest thrust his head out of the window. Even though he'd made this journey many times before, he never tired of the view. Stretching far below them through the haze, he could just make out the River Seddon, winding its way across the Gondarian Plain and in the distance Gonda, Durbah's capital and centre of the civilised world. You could go around the formidable barrier of the escarpment by following the River Seddon through a steep gorge to the east or travel west around its edge; it was much safer, but both roads entailed another three torturous days travelling. He thought to himself, *no, better to go directly this way; besides, he was not in any real danger*.

He heard Phipps calming the horses as the carriage disappeared beneath the dense canopy into the escarpment's twilight world and began its decent down the winding road, the all-pervading menace echoing with strange and exotic noises, the jangle of harnesses and rattling wheels sounding out of place in the heavy, humid atmosphere. Suddenly the squeal of brakes accompanied by the clatter of slewing hooves sounded in the stillness, and the carriage came to a grinding halt.

'Phipps, what's the matter?'

'I think we're being robbed, Sir.'

'Oh, is that so!' declared Almagest, stepping purposefully from the carriage to be met by a couple of scruffy, unshaven, leather-clad men armed with swords and crossbows.

'Save yourself some grief, old man,' said one. 'Get back in your carriage and hand over your valuables.'

'I shall only say this once; I am in a hurry and not in the mood for your games, for your own sakes I suggest you let us pass.'

'Oh, thinks he's a tough cookie, does this one, Charlie.'

'I think he needs to be taught a lesson in toughness, don't you Spanes,' and, levelling his crossbow, the man called Charlie aimed and fired - the bolt never reached its intended target, instead the wooden shaft of the bolt spontaneously exploded into feathers.

The two men looked sheepishly towards each other, then at Almagest. 'We may have made a mistake here, as you say. I think we'll be on our way…'

The bandit called Spanes moved no further as a large man suddenly appeared from the undergrowth and, producing a wicked-looking knife, slit the throat of Charlie and then thrust his knife, to the hilt, up through the other bandit's jaw and into his skull.

'Hogan?'

At just over eight feet tall and three hundred pounds, Hogan, the product of a union between human and outcast, glared across at him pitilessly from piercing brown eyes, set beneath thick, black, bushy eyebrows, framed by shortcut, greasy jet-black hair. Almagest watched as Spanes turned to look up at Hogan, the look in his dying eyes one of utter disbelief.

'Aye, Sir, are you alright?' said the giant man, letting the bandit drop to the floor, the life already gone from his eyes.

'Was that really necessary? I was in no danger.' Eyeing the bodies disdainfully as their life's blood pooled beneath them, Almagest said, 'I didn't know you were so proficient with a knife.'

'The product of a jaded past, Sir. Better to be safe than sorry, that's what I say.'

'What are you doing here, man?'

'On my way to Gonda I was; an errand for Alfic, you see; when some kind of animal attacked. My horse didn't survive.'

Struggling to placate the horses from his seated position, Phipps said uneasily, 'We need to go, Sir, the wildlife hereabouts can smell death from miles away.'

Turning towards the carriage, Almagest said, 'Fortunate for you then that we came along when we did.' Sensing an uneasiness and apprehension in Hogan, he asked, 'Are you alright? You seem distracted.'

'No, Sir, but, as your man said, we need to go.'

Suddenly clarity hit him. The bandit's look of disbelief wasn't because of the circumstance, but who had done it. Turning abruptly, Almagest didn't see the knife that flashed towards him, but he did feel the blade as it thrust upwards through his abdomen and up into his chest.

'Kuelack sends his regards,' grinned Hogan, with foul-stained teeth.

One-hundred-and-fifty years Almagest had been on this earth, through wars and uprisings, good times and bad, only to be played for a fool, deceived and killed by a half-wit giant, masquerading as one of the school's staff, sent by a mage less than half his age. Perhaps Kuelack was right after all, the Sivan and the school, the very institution had become indolent with conformity and perhaps he had paid for his arrogance with his life.

Before darkness took him, he watched, helpless, through blurring vision as Hogan, after a brief struggle, crushed Phipps's skull with a giant fist.

As his lifeblood stained the soil beneath him, Hogan loomed over him, his hand wielding the wicked-looking knife. He then felt a final shocking impact, then nothing.

CHAPTER SEVEN

YOU CAN CHOOSE
YOUR FRIENDS...

Yawning, her mind still fuzzy from yet another sleepless night, Magen struggled to sort through the problems her brother now presented. His neutralising of fellow council members, for instance, disposing of anyone who challenged or stood against him; even Ramus had made an attempt on her life. Realising she was out of her depth; she'd concluded her best option was to share her information with Alfic; he was clever and resourceful; he would know what to do. Alfic was also removed from the school and its politics.

Making her way through the school grounds, Magen closing the gate behind her, started out across the field, startling a parliament of feeding rooks and a small herd of roe deer that suddenly bounded towards the trees, flashing their warning with bright white bobbing tails.

Walking through the whirls of mist that rose from the warm earth into the chilly morning air, she watched the deep amber sun climb above the horizon through streaks of grey cloud. *The countryside always held a magical quality this early in the morning,* she mused. She had always intended to walk more frequently like she had as a child with Alfic and Perak, but time and duty had dealt her a tough hand. *Those were happy, carefree days, without responsibility, days it seemed the school would never see again should I choose not to act. Kuelack had never appreciated the simple pleasures of the world around him. The glorious sunrises or the clouds in the sky, the sheer beauty of a wood carpeted in Bluebells in bloom, to him these things were a waste of time, a sign of weakness.*

By the time she reached the cottage garden gate, she was sweating profusely from the arduous walk, and after she had caught her breath, she knocked on the door.

'Magen?' smiled Lascana. 'This is a pleasant surprise. What brings you here this early?'

'Lascana,' she smiled, 'is Alfic here?'

'Yes, he is, come in,' greeted Lascana, hugging her fondly, 'he's in the kitchen. I'll put the kettle on.'

On entering, Alfic, who was whittling at a piece of sycamore into a small dog with a penknife, greeted her.

'Sister, hello, to what do we owe this visit?' he said, studying her. 'My, my, we are out of shape. This must be the furthest you've travelled from the school in oh, ten years.'

'I'm not here to discuss my fitness, Brother,' she snapped. 'Or my travelling history.'

'My, my, someone got out of the wrong side of the bed this morning.'

'I'm not here to discuss my sleeping patterns, either. I have news that could well change the course of our lives and the future of the school. I'm also here to ask for your help.'

'OK,' said Alfic warily.

'Kuelack is planning to take over the school.'

'Take over the…?' smiled a disbelieving Lascana, nearly dropping a tray containing three cups and saucers on the dining table. 'Surely you're mistaken; his views may be a bit extreme and unconventional, but I can't believe he would plot against the school.'

'Well, I'm sure of it.'

'And you know this how?' asked Alfic.

She studied their astounded expressions for a moment before continuing. 'On returning to my apartment two nights ago, I overheard voices coming from Kuelack's quarters. There was no mistaking Mass's voice. Ramus and Kuelack's apprentice, Tallus, were there as well.'

'Why come to me with this problem, why not Almagest or Exedra?' asked Alfic.

'They have enchanted Exedra,' she said despairingly.

'Enchanted? What do you mean? By who?'

'By Mass Martin, also Almagest's been called away on a falsehood, and I believe his life is forfeit at the hands of your man Hogan who, far from a destitute farmhand in need of work, is an assassin working for Kuelack.'

'Almagest is the most powerful sorcerer we know, he wouldn't dare, he couldn't.'

'It's true, Lascana. I overheard Kuelack mention his name. I've sent a messenger to find him but he hasn't returned either…' she left the rest unsaid.

'Anyway, the next day I tried to confront Kuelack, but Ramus intercepted me.' Tears welled up in her eyes as she relived the brief thirty seconds of terror. 'It was then that he attacked me.'

'Attacked you? What, with magic?' said Lascana, outraged. Rising to her feet, she announced, 'You... you're Magen Breed, a member of the Sivan.'

'Yes, and if it wasn't for Savarin... Look, I know I should be better than this. Ramus said the fight's gone from me, and he was right, it has,' she cried. 'For the past three days, I've been thinking about our encounter, going over it in my mind. I don't know what to do Alfic, I don't know what Kuelack will do,' she sobbed. 'That's why I came to you, Brother; you're my only ally, and the one person I can trust.'

Consoled by Lascana, Magen studied Alfic's sceptical face as he wrestled with the current information.

'It's not as far-fetched as it sounds and it would explain a lot; why Hogan's not turned up for work recently for one,' confirmed Alfic. 'At the time, Perak thought it was strange, Kuelack recruiting Hogan over and above his head. Now we know why. If Hogan has been sent to kill Almagest; and Almagest doesn't realise Hogan's true intent, he'll succeed...'

'Only the other day he was talking about the wizards of old, asking me if I would fight to protect the school and its traditions,' despaired Magen. 'I never thought...'

'Magen, you're fourth on the Sivan; with this evidence you could have Ramus and Mass arrested,' insisted Lascana.

'What evidence do I have, who can I truly turn to, Lascana?'

'Savarin would help you, as would Rasbora, surely?' suggested Lascana. 'They're next in line for the council table.'

'I don't want to start a war pitting teacher against teacher. Besides too many people are already involved in this madness, who knows how deep this conspiracy goes.'

Looking up suddenly, brow screwed up in puzzlement, Alfic said, 'These schemes didn't just form overnight; Kuelack must have been planning this for years. In light of this fresh evidence, it confirms what I've always suspected; that Torsk's untimely death wasn't an accident.'

'Ramus confirmed without actually saying anything that Cardia was also murdered by Kuelack.'

'And shortly after they voted Exedra onto the Sivan,' confirmed Lascana, rising from her chair at the insistent whistling of the kettle.

Magen smiled for the first time in days, having regained a modicum of security in her brother's presence. Despite her trepidation, she was glad she had sought him out as she watched him ponder this recent information; his aversion to injustice and his keen, inquiring mind working on the problems she had unearthed as he paced back and forth.

'So, can't we just convince Exedra of Kuelack's plot? She's even less forgiving than Almagest. If she found out, I'd pity Kuelack,' Lascana insisted.

'Lascana, the enchantment would be very subtle.'

'You are correct, Alfic. One word or action could trigger a command in her mind, harming her or us,' confirmed Magen.

'Did Ramus say anything else?'

'No, nothing – oh yes, he asked me to join him, fight against Kuelack. When I refused that's when he tried to kill me, said he couldn't risk me jeopardising his plans.'

'Jeopardise his plans, not their plans. Then he's got his own agenda. Maybe we can exploit that?' mused Alfic.

'There is one other thing,' said Magen meekly. 'Kuelack ordered the student Tallus to investigate this Dark Creature stalking the countryside.'

Burying her head in her hands, Lascana worried, 'Bloody hell; the Dark Creature! If Tallus investigates this thing, then it's a possibility, however remote, that he'll come across Aridain as Kale did. Then it's conceivable Kuelack could discover his secret, despite all of our safeguards.'

'Secret, Kale?' queried Magen, who sat staring at the pair sceptically.

Alfic and Lascana seemed to come to a silent agreement. Then, looking up at her in trepidation, Lascana said, 'There's a favour I would ask of you while you're here. As you know, they assigned Kale to investigate the magical anomaly...,' she began.

'Yes, that's right,' agreed Magen.

'The anomaly is a Dark Creature.'

Ignoring Magen's surprised expression, Lascana continued... 'Kale traced the Dark Creature to the woods behind us, the place where Aridain plays the most. Kale suggested that Aridain is attracting this creature.'

'That would mean Aridain has a gift that's...' Magen gasped, 'Let's just say it, immense.'

'Kale said the same. He found out because Vara wove a deflection spell over Aridain when he was born.'

'And looking for the creature drew him to the source and then the spell,' confirmed Magen knowingly.

'I know he's very young, Magen, but Aridain needs to learn how to suppress his magic and control it,' Lascana pleaded. 'Kale has offered but said, "the task was suited to someone with much more experience" and he mentioned you. Don't you see; if he found out, Kuelack would see Aridain as a threat in the future.'

'Or, as a future ally,' countered Magen.

'Maybe even try to use him against us? Let there be no doubt that we will not take chances where our son is concerned. No one will threaten him without answering to me!' vowed Alfic.

Throwing Alfic a harrowing stare, Lascana said, 'We're asking you to help keep our son safe. I cannot stand by and see him learn how to kill and destroy, his face bitter and twisted with malice and hate.'

'You don't have to ask; I will do it gladly.'

'Thank you and in return, Magen, we will both confront our brother and wring the truth from him.'

'No, Brother,' ordered Magen, 'You won't, I will. I am the eldest and more powerful sibling. He knows better than to attack me.'

'Are you sure you can do this, Sister?'

'I'm sure. Knowing I have your support is enough. You have both given me renewed confidence. Thank you.'

'Oh, before I leave there is one more thing; I didn't mention it because I didn't think it important, but Kuelack was also talking about the Firebrand stone.'

'What? Why would he do that?' exclaimed Alfic.

'I don't know but he said he had located it and that Pellagrin had lied; instead of destroying it, he'd split the stone into four pieces, then hid them. Ramus mentioned it as well. Do you think he was telling the truth?' questioned Magen.

'No, no, the very notion is ridiculous,' said Alfic unconvincingly. 'Pellagrin destroyed the Firebrand stone.'

'Magen, MAGEN!'

Having wandered across the fields and into the school grounds, Magen, jolted from her thoughts, looked up to see Beria standing in her way.

'Magen, I've been waiting for you,' said a concerned Beria. 'I tried to catch your attention earlier.'

'I had some important business to attend to. What is it?'

'Early this morning I saw someone acting strangely outside the Administration building, so I decided to follow.'

'And?' said Magen, irritably.

'He followed you from the Administration building when you went for your walk.'

'Following me?'

'Yes.'

The spring day had suddenly taken on the chill of winter as she pictured the figure crouched down outside Lascana's dining-room window, listening to every word they had said.

This person could be in Kuelack's office right now, retelling their entire conversation. Why else would this person be eavesdropping? She thought. It seems the fates have deemed that I confront Kuelack now.

'Thank you for telling me, Beria. Can you do me a huge favour and take my class?'

'What, now? What about my own class?'

'I know it's asking a lot, but it's important. Put them together or something. I have to go. I'll explain later,' shouted Magen as she hurried across the grass.

Mustering the courage she had gleaned from her meeting with Alfic, she entered the Administration wing and ascended the main stairway, walking guardedly to Kuelack's apartment located directly next to hers in the Keeps south wing, but when she raised her fist to knock, the door swung noiselessly inwards.

'Come in, Sister!'

Taking a deep breath, she entered his private office and, with as much composure as she could muster, approached her brother. Dressed in his crimson finery, Kuelack sat imperiously on his black and red onyx gold-inlaid, (and there was no other word for it) throne which stood behind his large, dark, stout wooden table. He stared at her in his smug, superior way, his hawk-like face pallid in the dimly lit apartment.

'Magen, come in,' he said, staring with cruel grey eyes from beneath dark vulture-like eyebrows and jet-black hair, swept back to the nape of his neck, 'you know Hogan, of course.'

Even though all the evidence pointed to Hogan working for her brother, she was still taken aback when, smiling humourlessly, the giant man spun around from his position at Kuelack's back.

In a deep, grating voice like the sharpening of a blade on a grindstone, Hogan rumbled, 'Mistress Magen'.

'I have it from a reliable source that someone followed me to Alfic's cottage,' she said with as much authority as she could muster. 'Who was it? Following and then eavesdropping on a teacher is a serious offence.'

'Yes indeed, Sister, and from what Ramus tells me, you're just as guilty,' Kuelack said with a wicked smile.

'Hogan, don't you realise that the only reason my brother would take pity on someone like you is that you are of some use? He doesn't really care about you; make a mistake and he will discard you like a piece of gnawed bone,' said Magen, staring at the bulky man who stood casually picking at his blackened teeth.

'Your talk with Alfic has given you courage, it seems,' said Kuelack. 'I admire cleverness, boldness and audacity, I do. But your efforts to place doubt in Hogan's mind will fall on deaf ears. You see, Hogan here tried to rob me a few years back, but he picked the wrong carriage. He knew he was going to get his neck stretched eventually, being a hunted man, and I needed someone who wouldn't ask questions and could carry out my orders ruthlessly and efficiently. Hogan knew a good deal when he heard one.'

'No more games, Brother. WHAT'S GOING ON?' she demanded. 'Did you order Hogan to kill Almagest? DID YOU?'

Kuelack looked up at her astutely. 'To the point. Very well, Almagest will not be joining us again, ever; he's on extended leave. Following a brief ceremony, I will be Head of this school. When the stone is in my hands, there will be no one to stop me.'

'Why do you keep talking about the Firebrand stone when you know it was destroyed?'

'I can see it in your eyes, Sister. You doubt your own conviction, despite what Alfic said, you realise what I say may be true.'

Magen smiled and shook her head resignedly. 'Fantasy won't help you, your plan to takeover this school will fail.'

'This school? My dear sister, my plans extend far beyond the school.'

Shaking her head wearily, Magen said, 'Anybody wanting to return to the "dark days", before Pellagrin sacrificed all to drive out the monstrosities let loose on the land, frankly need their head examined. Some parts of the world still haven't recovered.'

'That's why I'm offering you a chance to be a part of this new venture. Of all "my family", you, Magen have been the dearest and the kindest to me. You're powerful and you care about the school as I do. Together we can take over sympathetically, stealthily and with no fuss, no upheaval.'

'What makes you think I would ever want to join you or go along with this madness?'

'Why? Because, in this dangerous world, people meet with accidents.'

Her hand covered her mouth as the realisation hit her. 'Alfic was right, you killed Torsk,' she gasped, finding it hard to focus.

'My brother is annoyingly clever,' hissed Kuelack. He then looked up at Magen intently. 'Yes, I had him killed.'

'And Cardia?'

'Disposed of,' said Kuelack

'What's the difference between "disposed of" and "killed"?' asked Magen, glancing at Hogan.

'Wasn't me!' shrugged Hogan, who smiled indifferently, the effort making him look like a grinning walrus.

'They were poking their noses into my affairs, and besides, they were weak, and not worthy of a place in my new regime. To succeed you have to separate the chaff from the wheat.'

With her brother's image swimming before her and finding no reason for her stupor, Magen attempted to clear her blurring vision and hissed, 'So, you're not as clever as you thought, Brother. They were about to expose your petty schemes.'

Kuelack jumped to his feet, slamming his fist on the table. 'You may be my sister, but take care in what you say.'

'I will not. I'm putting a stop to your insane schemes right now.'

With Kuelack defenceless, Magen gestured, certain her power would incapacitate him and Hogan instantly, but instead of a blister of force there was only a hollow emptiness.

'Did you honestly think I would be naïve enough to let you access your power in my quarters?' he said smugly. 'I was willing to give you the benefit of the doubt, but I had safeguards installed just in case.'

She grunted with pain and collapsed to the floor as, with a gesture, a smiling Kuelack, raising his fist, slowly squeezed and then released her, much to Hogan's amusement.

'So now you see the futility of opposing me. I will tolerate no interference. You will join me, Sister, or suffer the consequences.'

'You can intimidate me all you like. Your threats mean nothing,' she quailed.

'Oh, I know,' said Kuelack treacherously, 'but what about your children, Magen? And Alfic's child, what about him?'

Wretchedly, she looked up at her brother from her position, knelt on the floor, his words striking her like a hammer blow. 'What sort of monster are you? Threatening the lives of our children; we're your family!'

He slammed his fist on the table. 'A monster who has the once great Magen Breed on her knees in front of him! Thanks to you, I now know all about Alfic's son and a power that you described as "immense". So, Magen, you will join me or they will suffer!' he said menacingly.

Trying desperately to focus her thoughts, Magen realised something in the air had prevented her from accessing her power. 'So, I have no choice?'

Indicating the school in general, he said, 'You must understand that I have a new family now, and this is my home.'

'Please Kuelack, if there is any pity left in your heart, don't punish our children,' she cried.

'Then swear allegiance to me.'

Desperately searching for something to say or do, Magen suddenly realised the helplessness of her position. She slowly looked up at her brother. 'I will... do as you ask.'

'Very good. If you co-operate, we shouldn't need to bother them at all.'

'So, all that you've said and done over the last few years was just a lie. Your work here with the students, your efforts on the school's behalf?'

'Oh no, my concerns for the school and its students are genuine. You see, Pellagrin's has lost its direction, its purpose. It's stagnating, stewing in its own bureaucracy. We have to conform; we must have a meeting for this and a meeting for that; Almagest's policies are pathetic.'

'It's called democracy.'

'It's pathetic, is what it is. No, it's time to put the school back on track. You and Almagest are a perfect example of its blight; your complacency, for instance, your lack of foresight.'

'And you think you're the man to do it?'

'I will establish the school as a centre of prominence, set the school, this province, on a path to greatness once more! Then when I unite the Firebrand stone, I will possess the power of a god, and only a god has the power to change destiny,' boomed Kuelack.

'I don't believe it; you actually believe what you're saying.'

'As for the lies, we will maintain them for now until I tell you otherwise.'

'Go back on everything I know to be true.'

'Yes, just tell Alfic you were mistaken.'

'He won't believe me and he won't trust me afterwards. Nobody will trust me,' she wailed.

'Oh, I think Alfic will trust you, after all you are going to instruct his son in the ways of magic as a shield against this creature.'

'Ply them with threats and lies, you mean,' cried Magen resignedly.

'Yes,' Kuelack said matter-of-factly. He glided quickly across the room and, seizing her by the collar, hauled her to her feet. 'You will instruct Alfic's son to think as we do and as our numbers grow, he will join us.'

'Alfic won't allow it.'

'Oh, I do hope so,' said Kuelack, letting her drop to the floor.

Rising unsteadily to her feet, she covertly scanned the room. There were many objects displayed on shelves and locked away in glass cabinets, but all were inactive. Then she saw the two glowing incense burners hanging from the ceiling beams above her head and realised that these, combined with Kuelack's dark power, were dampening her own.

'Took you long enough, Magen; my, my, we have become sloppy.'

She looked at her brother's self-righteous countenance through the enchanted smog. She had brought this situation down upon them. Her mind in turmoil, she desperately searched for something to do or say, still clinging to the hope that he would listen to sense. Then she realised miserably the reason she hadn't noticed the incense burners before. Kuelack was right; she'd become so accustomed to the idyllic life at Pellagrin's, so entwined in its fabric, that her mind simply refused to believe anything bad could happen. She had become complacent and indolent with conformity. As her eyes settled on the burners, she again felt his power wrapping her arms against her side.

'Your confusion will pass in time as you realise the truth of what we are trying to do.'

'So, you're going to find and unite the Firebrand shards and take over the world. Why?'

Kuelack appeared before her, grasping her chin firmly in his hand, and he turned her head to look up into his eyes. 'Once we restore the school to its former glory, the students under the most powerful teachers in the realm will follow us and together we'll make Durbah in the school's image. I've seen other lands sniggering and I've heard the rumours. The other kingdoms think this land has become an overstuffed warthog ripe for the slaughter. Well, I will make the other lands of Aymara respect Durbah once more. No one will ever disrespect or challenge us again. Never again will they take us for granted. The people of the other kingdoms will worship us.' He strolled around the room, his arms and hands moving in time with his words. 'Indulge me for a moment while I let you into a revelation I've had. I have concluded that the history books mask a great truth, that in fact Pellagrin wasn't a great man at all but a wizard afraid of his own abilities. I will go so far as to accuse Pellagrin of gross negligence in his responsibilities to the realm. If Pellagrin had believed in his own power, instead of splitting the stone, he could have easily wielded it. He could have ruled and moulded the land as he wished, into a world ruled by truly great men instead of bowing to the wishes of politicians and bureaucrats.'

'And the wicked and evil took care of its own,' whispered Magen, who shook her head in disbelief. Perhaps the legends were true; perhaps it was already too late. Wizards of old prophesied that even the thought of possessing the stone could corrupt a person's soul.

'You may threaten me into silence, but I will never agree with what you are doing,' she spat.

'Just consider the children, Magen Breed. Think of their healthy faces,' lectured Kuelack, sitting back down behind his desk. Then, with a contemptuous look, he released her. 'You will receive your orders soon. Now get out of my sight, Councillor.'

Turning with all the grace and dignity that she could muster, Magen staggered from the room, the door slamming shut behind her with an inevitable finality. As much as she felt like crying, the tears would not come through the drug-induced haze. Kuelack had denied her even that small indulgence.

CHAPTER EIGHT

DREAMCASTERS

A month had passed since he had given Kale the task of tracking down the Dark Creature, which had remained strangely illusive; strangely illusive because with plentiful signs of activity, i.e., the blight, which far from dissipating had continued to spread; he should have at least encountered it by now. But despite his continued forays into Farend woods and the surrounding countryside, he had only encountered animals. *It should be easy to find,* he thought frustratedly. *What am I missing?*

Irritably, and a mite frustrated, Kale closed the door to his classroom after another day trying to impress on his students the intricacies and nuances involved in the art of becoming an Animistic, and what a privilege it was to communicate with the creatures of this world.

Most students were a joy to teach; some, however, were troublesome individuals, like Tallus Ramca, he thought, sidestepping a large puddle. It's hard enough trying to impart the teachings Torsk passed on to me without constant disagreements and interruptions, making a mockery of my methods. Trying to teach the elderly student was like a younger brother being put in charge of an older sibling while the parents were absent; the older brother would never conform.

Kale recalled a conflict earlier in the week… Tallus had stood up in front of the class and argued, "You cannot simply ignore rules; Kuelack teaches us that rules apply to many types of magic, even witchcraft. Spells will turn around and consume its conjuror if he or she has failed to follow the rules exactly. Dark magic especially demands a dear price."

He had tried to explain - 'I don't disagree, but some practices like Elemental, Natural, Weather and, to a degree, our own art, are only limited by your imagination. If your mind is too rigid, too inflexible, how will you ever manage to transform your state, change your form to fit the creature you want to imitate?'

"Are you disagreeing with the greatest Mage Pellagrin's has ever known in front of the class? And after he put his faith in you?" came the retort.

"Kuelack is not an animistic. If you want to master our art, his teachings will only hasten failure on your part."

Storming from the room, Tallus had fumed, "Master Kuelack's teachings are second to none, and his students are devoted to him. He will hear of your 'opposition'."

It was a mistake, Kale knew, to question Kuelack's methods openly, and he feared the outcome of his outburst, but he would not allow Tallus to sully Torsk's teachings or his good name. He still missed his former tutor, who he'd regarded more like a father figure than a teacher, his reassuring demeanour always a balm when he doubted himself or his ability. No doubt he would have had some inspirational words for him in this time of uncertainty.

He hurried angrily past the many lecture rooms of the primary teaching building lit by shafts of amber sunlight lancing in through the vaulted windows. Students young and old, dressed in their white uniforms and assorted insignias, now released from the day's teachings, ran excitedly down the hallway, their voices and noisy footsteps echoing down the stone-floored corridor; most, no doubt, heading towards the kitchens. He wondered if they truly appreciated their surroundings, as he had as a young boy. On his first day of attendance, he could clearly picture Torsk standing behind his podium, relating the school and the building's illustrious history. While feeling more than a little scared as he had listened intently, the teaching block's welcoming atmosphere had seemed to embrace him.

Shading his eyes against the evening sunshine cascading in through the building's majestic, multi-coloured stone arched facade, he negotiated the wide spiral stairway to the ground floor. Skipping past one of the retainers muttering about the annoying habits of students while he mopped up a spill, he exited the classroom block through the large double doors that comprised the entrance and looked beyond the lengthy three-storey high building. In the sky beyond, yet another dark squall raced towards the school, threatening to block out the sun that threw the building's exquisite blue-leaded domes, dreamy spires and stately ornate chimneys into sharp relief. Confident he could make it to his meeting with Mace before the rain arrived; he strode purposefully beside the combat field, then turned left beside Seline's fountain on his way towards the kitchens.

As the wind intensified, students and teachers alike hurried back and forth as the skies once again darkened with the threat of rain. Passing beside the rugged walls of the main Keep, he ducked in through the Hall of Worship, the kitchen's smells now enticing him onwards. He reached the entrance just as the heavens opened; the clouds casting down small pebble-sized hailstones that clattered noisily from the rooftops. Upon entering the hall's warm, inviting atmosphere, Kale scanned the milling throng of people and students talking and laughing. Like busy termites, the staff waited upon tutors and pupils alike, serving platefuls of food amidst a background clatter of cutlery and china, and an atmosphere dominated by the fumes of cooking and pipe smoke.

Despite the squally weather everyone it seemed was in a good mood, everyone that was, except himself and Mace, who as he approached, stared glumly at the table, listlessly pushing around the contents of his untouched meal with his fork.

'What's the matter with you?'

Mace slammed his fist on the table, making the cutlery and unlit candleholder fly into the air and land back on the thick oak table with a clatter.

'It's this investigation; it's been a month, and we're no closer to killing this thing or discovering why it's tracking Alfic's family. They discovered two more bodies in the grounds opposite, gamekeepers both, with their clothes gone, their heads caved in, brains and hearts gone and bodies drained of fluids. It's like this creature's sucking out their very soul?' said Mace, shivering. 'Strangely, when I asked, "if any of the remaining staff had seen anything?" One man swore he saw a man called Celias Erkit leaving the scene.'

'Hold on, wasn't that the name of the first victim?'

'Yes, he was a former employee.'

'But that makes no sense; the only way they recognised him was by a tattoo. Talking of strange, I've found the carcasses of numerous animals on the grounds in a similar state, but no people. However, I did encounter a strange, sombre man, who when asked if he'd seen anything strange only shook his head and shambled off into the wood,' insinuated Kale, 'you don't think…?' He then looked up self-consciously as a plate of food was placed before him. 'Thank you, Amanda,' he said, forcing a smile towards the serving girl. He then sat back with a scowl on his face as Mace continued to brood and cast his mind back over the last few weeks to the people he'd met. People who had fled in terror having heard the creature's strange, haunting cry, which they described as the tortured shriek of a banshee. However, more worryingly, he knew it was only a matter of time, despite his reassurances, before people put two and two together and realised that the creature's face matched that of Alfic's son. Then superstition and fear of the unknown would drive these people to question why this was so, and those fears would inevitably cause trouble for the insightful grounds man and his family. Munching ravenously on a shank of lamb, Kale, after a long pause, asked, 'What do you think of Tallus?'

'Tallus? Tallus Ramca? He's not interested in the combative arts, but I know he's a firm follower of

Kuelack's. I also know that the two of you don't get on, as does the entire school.'

'The entire school!' exclaimed Kale, swallowing a large mouthful of food. 'Is it that obvious?'

Nodding vigorously, Mace smiled. 'Uh huh, that and the fact that Tallus has voiced his displeasure more than once at playing second fiddle to you.'

'I'm beginning to agree with him, for this is an art I'm only just starting to explore.'

'Torsk named you as his successor for a reason. He entrusted his class to you for a reason. Look, you've told me yourself; Tallus's methods are, shall we say, dubious? Do you think he's talented enough to attract this creature?'

'No, and neither is any other student…' slurped Kale, wiping his mouth with the back of his hand while manoeuvring a piece of bread through the gravy-filled plate. 'I've been tracking this thing for nearly a month, Mace, and nothing,' said Kale despairingly. 'It's like trying to catch smoke in a fishing net. I've even visited the library to explore what combination of magic it would require to conjure such a creature, so far without success.'

'But you intend to find out, right?' finished Mace, staring in astonishment at Kale's empty plate.

'Yes. I have an idea about how to do that. And you?'

'Oh, I'm more determined than ever,' smiled Mace. 'There's definitely something going on here. I've had a word with Keegan asking him to keep an eye on Hogan and, in the meantime, I will keep an eye on Ramus. Did you even taste that going down?' queried Mace, eying his plate.

Kale nodded deliberately. 'When I'm anxious, I eat. I might even go back for seconds!'

Strolling across the combat field fondling his badge of office, Kuelack watched the grunting students as they hacked and slashed at each other in barbaric fashion. He embraced the cool breeze that caressed his face and head of dark black hair; whipping the leaves from the sodden earth forming swirling vortexes and swirled the ends of his cloak out behind him. The earthy aromas stirring memories of his childhood; memories of his walks together with his brother and sister on Spalding Common, their father pointing out birds, insects and squirrels that scurried and scampered about the branches of a familiar giant, gnarled, wind-blown oak tree.

Clambering into its branches one fine autumn day, Alfic had called for him to join him. So, with his father's help, he had grasped one of the lower branches and followed his brother into the tree.

'Race you to the top.'

But as hard as he tried, he could not catch his brother who, like the squirrels he mimicked, raced ahead.

'I think we should climb down now,' he had shouted uneasily, clinging to the creaking bough. 'It's really high and it's getting windy.'

'Oh, don't be a coward. Father says this tree has stood for hundreds of years in the wind and rain. He says oak wood is the strongest there is.'

As he had climbed higher and the branches swayed precariously in the wind, fear had gripped him and he froze.

'Are you all right, Kuelack?' Perak had called.

'I'm fine, Father.' He had cursed angrily. But he hadn't been all right. While his brother, undaunted, had climbed higher and higher, he had clung to the branch with tears in his eyes.

'Don't panic, Kuelack, it's alright,' shouted Perak. 'I'll come and get you.'

He remembered Perak reaching him then, with encouraging words, guided him down through the branches as he whimpered and cried. When he reached the ground, Perak had tried to tell him that people were not all the same, that some people were better at different things; but all he kept thinking about was that it was Alfic's fault; that he'd done it on purpose; that he'd tricked him into climbing the tree.

Sensing Tallus's approach across the field, Kuelack, shaking himself from his thoughts, turned and waited for the young Animistic to join him. He then walked beside the grassy bank that flanked the combat field, with Tallus following a respectful step behind.

'Tell me, did you examine the bodies?'

'Yes, Master.'

'And?' he said irritably.

'Heads and hearts missing and drained of all fluids; the creature is feeding.'

'And?' he snapped irritably. 'Have you seen it?'

'Yes, briefly. It moves during the night. From what I saw, its face bears an uncanny resemblance to Alfic's son. It has a dull black wiry body, very much like a Wildling Outcast, and leaves a decaying stain wherever it touches.'

'Elaborate.'

'This creature is returning to the woods behind your brother's cottage; but to what purpose I have yet to determine, however, its resemblance to Aridain is more than just coincidence.'

'Continue?' snapped Kuelack irritably.

'I tried to scan the child as you asked.'

'And what did you find out?' asked Kuelack, forebodingly.

'Nothing, something prevented me.'

'So, the celebrated Tallus Ramca failed, defeated by a six-year-old boy.'

'To my shame, yes, so I tried to scan the Dark Creature's mind; it's something I will not attempt again.' He shivered, 'Its mind is vile and depraved.'

'Yes, I can imagine,' replied Kuelack, enigmatically. He then turned to look into the eyes of the young Animistic. 'Something on your mind?'

'This creature, Master, is an abomination and needs killing. Just say the word, and I will summon something that will rid us of it for good. It could become a serious threat.'

'It is of no concern; besides, I fear your meddling will only end in your death. No, I want you to monitor only. If the creature is connected to Alfic's son, I will discover why.'

'But, Master, I think you should seriously reconsider. If you would allow me to prove my worth, let me kill it…'

'Don't be foolish!' Calming himself with an effort Kuelack continued, 'One day, Tallus, you will realise that patience, subtlety and caution can be powerful weapons, as can information, and that action isn't always the right path to take, besides, Magen has it in hand.'

'Yes Master, you are wise as always.'

'As long as we know where these strange look-a-likes are we'll bide our time, then once the shards are in my hands Alfic's son and this creature will be mine.' Kuelack narrowed and then closed his grey, angular eyes and came to a decision. 'Eliminate Kale Simm and then take over the investigation. Make it seem as if that "thing" did it. I'll leave the details to you.'

Tallus smiled wickedly. 'I thought you'd never ask. Master, what about Mace Denobar and the gamekeeper, Keegan?'

'Those particular problems are in hand. You have another question?'

'Yes, Master, your brother; I am concerned as I have heard stories of his tenacity in pursuing the truth.'

'It's in Alfic's nature to stand up to me,' said Kuelack calmly. 'The one person he will suspect is at the heart of the trouble. Do not fear, Alfic's fighting days are behind him; I am the superior brother now. When he confronts me, he will lose. As for the staff and the teachers, they will have no choice but to embrace the future I have planned for the school. If not, they will die.'

'Kale, over here!' shouted Keegan through the evening mist. 'I think you should see this.'

Striding purposefully across the barley field, through the deepening gloom, towards the grey shapeless form crouched next to the fence line, Kale replied, 'How did you know it was me? I could have been the creature for all you know!'

'You make a particular sound when you move.'

'I wasn't making any sounds!' said Kale indignantly.

'Don't feel bad, it's what I do best.'

'What have you there?' inquired Kale irritably.

'Pheasants, or what's left of them.' Pulling his knife from the sheath on his bicep, Keegan thrust it into one of the pheasant's carcasses and laid it upon a grassy tussock for Kale to study. 'I reckon it killed them last night.'

'Let me look. This is not the creature. This is new,' confirmed Kale, closing his eyes and waving his hands over the carcass. 'You see this small hole?'

'I did wonder.'

Kale looked at Keegan in surprise. 'Whatever it is, it drained the pheasant's bodily fluids through this.'

'Like an insect?'

'An insectide magic feeder.'

'A what?'

'Everything is infused with magic, Keegan, to varying degrees, from a Brine Flea to a Zapatain Rock Dragon. I have an idea what it may be, but I won't speculate as these things haven't been seen around here for generations.'

'You sure know how to cheer up a guy. Come on, it's getting late, let's get you settled in for the night,' bemoaned Keegan.

Walking back across the misty fields in the evening's half-light they watched in mute fascination as a barn owl, gliding on gossamer wings, swooped, then emerged from the orchard's edge with a vole clasped in its talons.

'Look at them!' Keegan said despairingly, as rabbits and crows fed undaunted on the barleycorn. 'They continue to feed bold as you like, despite all our efforts.'

'Keegan, I'm sorry I insisted on this… but when you told me Tallus had been practising in the fields behind the dormitories, I didn't think telling him it was against the rules was going to cut it,' teased Kale.

'Hey what are friends for? Besides, I don't mind company now and again. Watching weird and wonderful creatures come and go, although highly entertaining during the dark evenings, can lose its allure after a time,' smiled Keegan cheekily.

Passing the periphery of the orchards and with the farm buildings to their left, they descended through a stand of barleycorn towards the track. This led to Keegan's shack, which sat on wooden piles and straddled the stream that fed two large lakes.

'A Korda knife. How did you come by that?' said Kale suddenly, eyeing the assassin's knife in its leather scabbard on his bicep. 'I've read those Calabashian assassins are damn nigh impossible to kill.'

'It's a memento.'

'How did you get it?'

'In the army.'

'You were in the army?'

'Yes,' said Keegan, 'together with Alfic and Mace.'

The next morning, Kale, stretching and yawning loudly, complained, 'What is that awful droning sound?'

'Oh, it's just a swarm of Hornet flies.'

'Hornet flies!' exclaimed Kale, sitting suddenly upright.

'Yes, they've gathered on the porch, around the wind chimes.'

Vigorously rubbing at his face to clear the fog of sleep, Kale said, 'I'm glad you're so calm about it.'

'Breakfast?' asked Keegan cheerfully.

Yawning again, Kale, slightly more composed, said, 'Yes, please. Talk about bad luck. I've sat here for four days and Tallus hasn't reappeared.'

Looking at Keegan as he rekindled the embers in his small stove, Kale held a newfound respect and even trepidation towards the enigmatic gamekeeper. The previous night, Keegan had regaled tales of his, Alfic's and Mace's past while sat drinking a bottle of Sorin's home brew. According to Keegan, before Mace had become a Greysword and Alfic a captain of the school guard, the three friends had belonged to an elite infiltration unit; regularly crossing the border into Calabash territory, gathering information on troop and cavalry movements as well as the secretive state's mages. Keegan hadn't specifically mentioned how many Korda they'd killed, but Kale had surmised it was quite a few. It was a testament to their skill as a team and their lasting friendship that they'd never been caught, unlike others of their unit.

Satisfied the fire was drawing nicely and feeding crumbs of toast to his ferrets through the bars of their cage, Keegan said, 'It's not bad luck. He knew we were here.'

'When did you figure that out?'

'Oh, a couple of days ago but guessing he knew this; I said nothing, figuring he'd think we'd move on. I was wrong. We will not find out anything else sat here.'

'Thanks for sharing,' said Kale sardonically.

'Oh, it's my pleasure,' chuckled Keegan.

'To think I spent four nights cooped up in this mess for nothing,' he grumbled. 'To say you're not house-proud is an understatement! How you ever find anything, I'll never know. It looks as though a maddened Ardent wolf has run amok in here. What have you done with my clothes?' he demanded.

'Oh, there…, over there under the window, I think.'

'Why…? Oh, never mind.' Grumbling under his breath, Kale found a pair of socks and tiptoed across the wooden floor to the window in his underwear; trying to avoid boxes full of fishing tackle and animal traps, as well as various items of clothing strewn around the cramped room. Having found his clothes and dressed, Kale chuckled.

'Something amusing?' asked Keegan; producing a couple of goose eggs and some bread.

'Just something Mace said.'

'Oh, and what was that?'

'He said you couldn't find a Firedrake in here if it burnt your backside,' laughed Kale, 'but your ferrets live like royalty. King Pheronis would be happy to live in those cages.'

'Hey, it may be a mess, but it's my mess,' Keegan said with a grin.

'You know I will never understand your desire to be on your own,' said Kale, motioning to the outdoors in general.

'I prefer the company of animals and to be at one with nature, OK? Animals don't argue back and they always let you know where they stand; unlike people, they have no hidden agendas,' declared Keegan. 'Being out here means not having to attempt to be sociable, or put on any airs and graces.'

'What about companionship?'

Keegan shook his head. 'I bed the occasional woman but decided long ago against relationships, they're hard work, besides I enjoy being the only person I have to worry about. In the army it was "kill the enemy or be killed"; it's the reason I never settled down or had children of my own. I couldn't have a family worrying whether I would return or was lying dead in a ditch somewhere, it's not right.'

'You're not in the army now,' challenged Kale.

'I guess I've become use to a life beholden to no one. Personal freedom is what life's all about for me now.'

Keegan made a hot pot of coffee and toasted some bread against his wood burner while Kale, finding Keegan's telescope, popped the end covers off and peered through the eyepiece. Scanning the fields, he watched Elias Tan, the school's baker, urge his horse, Drummer, up the incline, as it pulled his wagon full of grain towards the school; then panning further around he watched Elimi and his brother, Elgin, spread lime over the nearest field. With no sign of Tallus, Kale returned the telescope and sat down with Keegan to eat and drink his cup of tea. 'In the next half an hour I've a feeling the school will be shrouded in mist.'

'Magic?'

'No, very warm moist air,' smiled Kale. 'Oh, by the way, the hornet flies are still outside.'

'Can't you get rid of them?' said Keegan, peering out at the growing swarm.

Kale looked back blankly.

'This is your area of expertise, after all,' insisted Keegan.

'Do you know what level of control I'd need to manage an insect swarm? Hundreds of individual creatures with barely a mind between them; as far as I know only Torsk could manage that feat.'

'Some creature teacher you are,' jested Keegan, rolling his eyes. Purposefully getting to his feet and throwing his utensils into a large ceramic bowl full of water, Keegan then strapped his knife around his bicep and a crossbow across his back.

'We're not going into battle, Keegan.'

'You can never be too careful, coming?' Keegan then tied his large utilitarian cloak around his shoulders and climbed out through one of the windows that looked out onto the stream.

Accompanied by the lonely bleat of sheep as they called anxiously to each other in the gloom, Kale followed Keegan out the window and up the bank behind the cabin. They then passed the mill built among the loose stands of trees, the groaning and clunking of the large oak-built sails sounding strangely eerie in the gathering mist. Walking silently along the path and over the stone bridge, they emerged into the mist-shrouded fields. Navigating the soggy margin of the smaller of the two ponds; they looked across towards Keegan's wooden hut, with its thatch-covered roof and single chimney.

'They're gone?' said Keegan.

'What are?'

'The hornet flies.'

'So…'

'A bit of a coincidence, don't you think? I feel Tallus is watching us?'

'That's got me thinking.'

'Careful now,' joked Keegan, maintaining a serious face.

'Tallus, like most humans, operates during the day; but most of the encounters with the creature, apart from Aridain's, have been during the night,' said Kale. 'I'm wondering; perhaps it doesn't like sunlight? So, in order to move during daylight, it somehow becomes its victims.'

'What gave you that idea?'

'It was something Mace said. He said they found all the victims naked, and that one of the dead was seen walking.'

'I don't know Kale, it's a hell of a leap.'

'Keegan, you'd surely notice a man walking around with half his head missing… What was that, did you hear that, Keegan? Keegan…?' He spun around to find the gamekeeper lain amongst the grass with a serene, almost drug-induced look on his face. 'KEEGAN!'

'Whoa, Kale, take it easy? It's a warm sunny day.'

'Warm sunny… Keegan, we can't see more than twenty feet in front of us,' insisted Kale, as he shook the gamekeeper's shoulders vigorously.

'Relax, stop shouting; rest for a bit.'

'Keegan!' he shouted, slapping his friend's face hard.

'Hey, steady on, Kale!'

Grabbing Keegan by the arm, with a supreme effort, he hauled the heavier man to his feet. It was then that he sensed it; the swirling smattering of an illusion blended

DEAN G E MATTHEWS

into the murkiness, accompanied by a fluttering sound approaching through the mist. Kale looked up suddenly as four emerald-skinned hawk-sized insects appeared through the mist, their pincer-like jaws snapping rapidly.

'Dreamcasters,' spat Kale.

'Interesting. You know of our kind. Even more surprising, you've resisted our enchantment.'

'Oh yes, I've heard of you.'

'Then you know resistance is futile.'

'I won't allow you to harm me or my friend.'

'Your words are of no consequence; soon both of you will be dead and we will feast on your flesh.'

Then, with claws and teeth bared, the four emerald green creatures flew towards him.

While he half carried / half dragged the reluctant gamekeeper to his feet, Kale hollered in desperation, 'We have to go. Help me here, Keegan; these things are trying to kill us.'

'Kill us, are you mad?' said Keegan as he wrenched his arm away. 'These are my friends.'

'That's what they want you to believe. For Gronin's sake, man, it's an illusion!' gasped Kale.

'You never used to be this prickly?' questioned Keegan vaguely.

'Now I know you're not yourself,' said Kale as he stared at his friend bizarrely.

Bobbing and weaving a few feet in front of him, their thin antennae twitching in anticipation, the Dreamcasters attacked. Drawing Keegan's Korda knife from its sheath, Kale swept it in a wide arch just as they reached him and felt it slice through hard carapace.

'*Curse you human, you're depriving us of our food,*' came the insect's injured thoughts.

'You think so, do you?' growled Kale, who, having gained a brief respite, stood in front of Keegan holding the wicked-looking blade out in front of him. He could feel the Dreamcasters combined assault on his mind and in desperation, searched for inspiration. Then in his mind's eye he found it, Torsk's words. *Do not doubt your abilities; it only reinforces your doubts; like the snake that eats its own tail, the circle is never ending.*

He had never attempted to control creatures so malevolent, let alone four of them, but he had to try; it was their only chance. Taking a deep breath, he closed his eyes and concentrated.

'*Is that the best you can do? How pitiable.*'

As the creatures approached with teeth and claws bared, Kale concentrated, now determined to counter these creatures' wanton disregard of his worth. Slowly at first, then accentuated with intricate hand movements, he penetrated their illusions and then their defences, slowly grasping and then squeezing their tiny minds. To his relief, the Dreamcasters, no more than an arm's length from him, began convulsing and shuddering as if in the throes of a seizure. Straining with the exertion, beads of sweat appearing on his brow, Kale slowly drew them close as if they were in the grasp of a giant invisible hand. With teeth clenched resolutely, he transmitted his thoughts to them: *Listen to me very carefully. You have made a big mistake by attacking us. Tell me why you are here. Your kind abandoned this area centuries ago. Why are you here?*

'*Magic too strong to resist!*' their exquisite minds shrilled. '*Compelled to obey!*'

'*Compelled by whom, another Animistic?*'

Kale liked to avoid trouble if he could, but then someone summoned these creatures here; that someone wanted them dead, and he had a good idea who. So, he squeezed their tiny minds harder, squeezed until the four creatures squirmed among the long grass in agony, but as hard as he tried the name would not reveal itself, his mind encountering only silence.

As a gentle and caring lover of all things in their infinite variety, he was loath to cause them any harm, so releasing them he warned, *Be gone from here, Dreamcasters, leave and never return, and if I catch you on the school's grounds again, I won't be so lenient.*

Freed from Kale's grip, the four Dreamcasters fled into the surrounding fog.

'Why am I down here on the wet grass?' asked Keegan, feeling the back of his breeches.

'Just give me a minute,' Kale said tetchily, wiping at the trickle of blood that ran from his nose and ears, then, taking a deep breath, he grasped Keegan's shoulder. 'Dreamcasters – four of them,' he panted. Keegan looked back at him blankly.

'You may know them as Harvestmen.'

'Harvestmen!' exclaimed Keegan, jumping to his feet and suddenly looking around concernedly.

'Calm down, they're gone. It seems someone wants us out of the way. The Dreamcasters' opposition told me what I wanted to know; that another, powerful mind has drawn them to the school, that person can only be Tallus.'

CHAPTER NINE

SECRETS AND LIES

It was now early summer and the rainsqualls that had raced in from the south, saturating the school and the countryside over the past week, had blown through and just as quickly petered out; the moisture evaporating from the paths in the early morning sunshine in whirls of vapour, akin to ephemeral snakes.

Following a hard morning's work, Perak was content just to sit on the soft grass of the Recreation Field. Taking a long swallow of water, he watched as students sat idly talking or fooling around, as students do, then, lying back and feeling the damp seep through his clothing, he rested his hands behind his head. His stomach rumbling his mind drifted back to earlier that same day...,

Having dressed and checking that he had everything he would need for the day ahead, he had opened the door intent on a hearty breakfast. Instead, he'd come face to face with a concerned-looking Beria who, with fist poised to knock on the door, looked furtively left and right.

'Beria, what are you doing here this early; are you alright?' he had asked, having seen the disquiet in her eyes.

'I need to talk to you,' she had insisted anxiously.

'I'm about to have breakfast; let's discuss your concerns over a strong, hot cup of tea.'

Beria, having agreed grudgingly, had accompanied him for the short walk from the accommodation wing to the kitchen. The kitchen was deserted apart from two members of staff and a hooded stranger who sat quietly sipping at a hearty broth. Ordering breakfast, they had collected their piping hot tea from the bar and sat down.

'So, Beria, what concerns you so much that you would come knocking at my apartment door this early?'

'A month ago, I followed a lone figure that had tracked Magen to Alfic's cottage. On her return, I confronted Magen about this suspicious behaviour. When I told her someone had followed her, she asked me to take her class. She didn't say why, but it seemed important. Ever since then she's not been herself.'

'"Not been herself", have you tried asking her why?'

'Of course I have, but she denies anything's wrong, saying that I'm imagining things. Magen's my friend Perak, I know when something's wrong.'

He had nodded knowingly. 'You kept this to yourself? You didn't tell anyone else?'

Beria looked up at him abruptly. 'Of course not, my concerns were for Magen.'

He looked up abruptly, roused from his recollections as loud voices encroached upon his thoughts, he then watched as a group of students armed with small wooden clubs, some riding piggyback, ran back and forth across the grass passing a small leather ball to each other. He smiled contemplatively, wondering if Aridain would get the chance to emulate himself and Alfic by playing in the school's Cabala team. Then, closing his eyes once more, his thoughts returned to his meeting earlier that morning.

'Beria, I'm only telling you this because Magen's your childhood friend and I believe you to be trustworthy. Magen was visiting Alfic to discuss certain issues she had concerning Kuelack. With Alfic's blessing, she was going to confront him. I'm guessing this person you saw must have overheard, followed and reported this meeting to Kuelack.'

He had watched as a range of emotions had played out across Beria's face.

'Report the meeting to Kuelack; to what end?' Beria asked, flabbergasted. 'What did Magen overhear?'

'She overheard him say he knew the location of the Firebrand shards. She also said his goal was to take over the school, and that his ambition was even greater than that.'

'You can't be serious; the stone was destroyed!'

'So we believed, now however….'

Perak had watched Beria's sceptical expression as the knowledge had sunk in, heard the disbelief in her voice as she had said, 'If what you say is true, that would mean…'

'My family are now in great danger, not to mention this school, all because Kuelack knows everything Magen, Alfic, and Lascana discussed,' finished Perak. 'If this knowledge disturbs you then walk away now and we'll speak of this no more?'

Squaring her shoulders and breathing deeply, Beria had nodded resolutely. 'You keep saying we, who are we exactly?'

A shadow blotted out the sun, rousing Perak from his musings once again, and shading his eyes, he looked up to see a tall stout figure outlined against the sun.

'Tad,' he smiled drowsily, 'you've done a good job; the grass looks so much better! We can't have dignitaries stepping in sheep droppings all week now, can we?'

'Not to mention the smell,' smiled Tad, screwing up his chubby face that reminded Perak of a tubby, wirehaired Bulldog. 'I can't wait for the fair,' he said, rubbing his hands together excitedly. 'All those rides and stalls, not to mention…'

'Let me guess, the girls,' finished Perak. Seeing Tad's astonished look, Perak said, 'I was young once,' he smiled, 'don't look so shocked, besides, we need some good cheer around here.'

Nicknamed Tad, Perak liked the young Nailer Tadman who, not endowed with the brightest of minds, worked hard nonetheless to send money back to his mother and sister in the village of Barfleet, his violent father having died in a drunken knife fight at the local tavern years ago.

Then, his demeanour turning decidedly frosty, Tad despaired, 'Oh, great!'

Following the chunky farmhand's gaze, Perak looked towards the great bulk of Hogan, striding across the field towards them.

Like a Basilisk sizing up a Jackrabbit for lunch, Hogan stood looking down at them ominously, and sneered, I've been instructed to report to you.'

Paying no attention to Hogan's attempt at intimidation, Perak stared up at the large man who, not moving, stared down at him with unveiled disdain.

'Is that so?' replied Perak with a grin and, pointing to a stack of timber at the far end of the field, he ordered, 'Then you can start erecting the stalls. The tools are there, we'll be along shortly,' insisted Perak. 'Well, what are you waiting for; get to it.'

In the school's current climate there was not a lot they could do without solid proof but convinced that Almagest was dead and that Hogan had done the deed, Perak had approached the large half man, half giant a few days earlier. Recalling the meeting;

'Tell me, Hogan, you wouldn't happen to know of Almagest's whereabouts, would you? You see, they summoned him to the capital on urgent business and no one's heard from him since.'

'I didn't know that,' Hogan had replied indifferently. *'You know what the headmaster's like, always off on one trip or another, leaving the running of the school to others.'*

Back in the present, Perak watched Hogan lumber away across the field.

Tad shook his head dejectedly. 'Oh, what fun I'm going to have this afternoon.'

Not scared of any man, Hogan had learnt that if you opposed the Dark Mage, there were far worse fates than death, so when ordered by Kuelack to help Perak erect the stalls and maintain the status quo, he dared not disobey.

It was an attempt to alleviate suspicion regarding their recent activities; an attempt to placate the dark Mage's family and to keep him occupied, thought Hogan scathingly, stomping frustratedly across the field. *Taking orders from Kuelack is a matter of survival, but Perak…? I shouldn't have to take orders from him or work with a bunch of ingrate weaklings, who I could crush with my little finger. We should... I should crush them all now; have it all over and done with; put the sheep out of their misery. It would be a simple matter; besides, we'll have to eliminate them soon, anyway.*

Two years previously, he had hidden with his gang in the dirt, waiting for their next victim in the rain-soaked night. However, that night on the main road to Feldspar town in the southwest of Durbah, his luck had run out. Having witnessed his men ruthlessly cut down as they approached one more ornately decorated carriage, he had attempted to escape, seized in an invisible fist of force and dangled upside down outside the carriage; but he wasn't destined to die that night. Instead, he had experienced genuine terror as Kuelack had looked into his very soul with savage steely grey eyes, and gave him an ultimatum; work for him and share in real power, or perish there and then. Later that night, while he sat in the Jewel and Diamond Inn in Feldspar's high street, he had pledged his service to the Dark Mage.

Concentrating on the task at hand, he scanned the stack of timber at his feet and began sorting them into roof, walls and base timbers. 'I still don't see why we have to bide our time,' he muttered under his breath. 'We have the power and the people in place to carry out the Master's plans, right here and now.' He suddenly looked up as Nailer Tadman approached across the field.

Ahhh! Things are picking up, he thought. *This afternoon's work won't be all doom and gloom after all.*

'GRAND POP!'

Hearing a familiar voice, Perak smiled, as approaching through the raucous crowd of students was Aridain accompanied by Lascana, the young bundle of energy launching himself towards his outstretched arms.

'Hello, young-un,' smiled Perak, squeezing Aridain in his arms. Then, standing up, he kissed Lascana. 'It is good to see you both, we need cheering up,' he said, inclining his head toward Hogan.

'Ahh, I see what you mean.'

'Grand Pop, we're here to help you with the fair,' announced Aridain proudly, looking up at him excitedly.

Lascana smiled. 'We thought between the two of us we could at least add up to another pair of hands.'

'Daddy?' shouted Aridain and ran towards his father as Alfic strode towards them through the throng of students, a resolute look on his face. With him were the brothers, Elimi and Elgin, looking decidedly subdued and red-faced.

Hugging his son, Alfic said, 'Hello, Father, I thought I'd bring some help. I found these two lounging around in the kitchens while others were doing their share of the work.'

Perak stared forebodingly at the freckled-faced Pike brothers. 'Don't just stand there like startled Jack Rabbits! Go and keep Tad company.'

'But can't we…'

'Go!' he bellowed, instantly regretting his tone.

The chastised brothers fled across the field towards the sheds.

'Don't worry, Grand Pop,' said Aridain knowingly, 'your bees can look after themselves for now.'

Rolling her eyes, Lascana, producing a piece of chalk and a measuring stick, took Aridain by the hand and led him away, saying, 'You young man, can help me mark out where the stalls are going.'

Frowning, Perak said, 'Come on, Alfic, the hands need saving from Hogan.'

Leaving the noise and chaos of the students behind, Alfic stated, 'You look tired, Father.'

He shook his head sorrowfully. 'It's not the work I mind, after all it gets me out of the house, it's the cupboard-sized room, with its matchbox single bed and dolls' house furnishings I can't stomach. I gave up trying to sleep days ago. Who'd have thought that the man, who as a child used to sleep on a straw covered floor, would actually miss the space and luxury that his own home provided. Luxury makes you weak, softens you up. Believe it or not, I even miss Vara, despite her sullen silences.' Watching as Aridain, giggling and shouting, ran with the measuring stick to a point dictated to by Lascana, he added. 'Vara's probably in seventh heaven now, revelling in the space and solitude.'

'I tell you, Father, Lascana and I are a bag of nerves,' stated Alfic abruptly. 'With this creature on our doorstep we're afraid to leave Aridain on his own and this may sound strange but I've a constant feeling we're being watched.'

'Then you won't like what Beria told me earlier.'

'Oh.'

'She told me when Magen visited your cottage someone followed her.'

'Followed?'

Perak nodded solemnly. 'Also, that over the past month Magen has been acting strangely. Now, considering they were best friends at school…'

'Magen only came to me because she was unable to cope with circumstances escalating beyond her control. I begged her to agree to both of us confronting Kuelack,' confirmed Alfic sadly, 'but she refused. It sounds to me like Magen has deferred to Kuelack's threats.' They both looked up guardedly as Tad approached.

'Tad, what can we do for you?' asked Perak.

'Can I have a word?'

Looking at Tad's normally jolly face, which had turned ashen, Perak inquired in a hushed voice, 'Of course Tad, what is it?'

'I'm just a grunt, a worker who wants a normal, quiet life,' sighed Tad. 'I've tried to get on with my work and avoid coming to you with this, but the threats and the intimidation are becoming more serious; it's not just me, it's Elimi and Elgin as well.

'Threats?' asked Alfic tentatively.

'Who's threatening you?' encouraged Perak. 'You can tell us, Tad.'

'Hogan and Tallus, they said that if I mentioned this to anybody, I'd rue the day. I don't know what they have against us; we've done nothing to them.'

'Ah ha… the reason for Elimi and Elgin's reluctance to work with Hogan,' nodded Alfic knowingly. 'That's why I found them in the bar.'

'Go on,' encouraged Perak.

'They asked if we'd "take on some important work" that we'd "be paid handsomely". When I asked what it involved, they wouldn't tell me, said I had to prove myself first, so I refused, but they won't take no for an answer.'

'It's OK, Tad,' Alfic said, calmly. 'Remember you have friends here; people who will help you if you'll let us.'

Tad nodded and breathed a huge sigh. 'Thank you, I didn't know what to do or who to trust, it's just that when you're an ordinary worker being threatened by people with power, it makes you feel powerless.'

'It's the way of the bully, to make you feel so inadequate that you'll agree to anything to stop them bullying you,' said Alfic.

'Remember, Tad, people only treat you as you let them. To retain your dignity, sometimes the only way to stop the bullying is to fight fire with fire,' said Perak.

'Now wait a minute! Violence, is that absolutely necessary?' exclaimed Tad, swallowing deeply.

'Sometimes, yes,' growled Perak.

'It's alright for you to say, you were both in the army. People like me, who come from a poor family, what are we to do?'

They worked for the remainder of the morning, hammering nails and sawing wood; the only communication between them were shouted instructions to erect the stalls. All around, boisterous teenage voices mingled with the occasional lowing of cattle from the fields.

'Is Headmaster Almagest really dead?' asked Tad suddenly.

'Keep your voice down,' hissed Perak. Then, relenting, he said, 'We have to be very careful what we say and who we say it to. We have no proof, but we've reason to believe that Hogan is the assassin.'

Tad looked shamefaced for a moment; indecision etched on his face. 'You're going to do something, right?'

'For the moment, no. He and Tallus work for my brother and with Almagest's death he has control. If we try to accuse Hogan - Kuelack and his associates will just close ranks,' spat Alfic.

'So, you're going to do nothing, despite all the stories I've heard of your family fighting for the common folk?'

'There are times to fight, but now is not one of them. If we provoke him the whole school may suffer the consequences.'

Tad turned away and looked as if he was going to be sick. 'I came to you thinking you could put an end to this.'

Gripping his shoulder and looking into his eyes, Alfic said, 'It took guts to come to us, Tad. The world would be a less dangerous place if there were more people like you, who stood up to be counted. Don't despair and don't give in to their threats.'

'And don't trust anyone until you're sure about them,' added Perak.

That night, hidden in the shadows next to the tool sheds, Keegan listened intently as Hogan spoke in harsh whispers with two burly youths. He assumed they were students, but with only starlight to light the way recognising their faces was impossible from his position hidden in the darkness. He then watched as Hogan, dismissing the figures, disappeared back towards the school.

Over the last few days Keegan had built up an admirable respect for the big man, following him patiently as he conducted his affairs with cunning and guile, watching silently as he met with Tallus and other students who he assumed were supporters of Kuelack. However, as impressive as Hogan was, he was better. During his vigils, sat silently in the dark, his thoughts had turned to Kale. For the past month, ever since their fateful encounter with the Harvestmen, he had become withdrawn, abandoning his investigations and not turning up at school, despite Keegan's efforts to find out why.

Setting his friends' problems aside, Keegan followed the two youths as they set off across the combat field; creeping along the bank below the copper beech trees until he was level with the procession of large chestnut trees, Keegan, with the grace of a stalking Virion cat, melted into the shadows. Scanning the darkness to check if they were being followed, the two students approached a lone figure silhouetted in the light of several torches, parrying and thrusting with a sword, using a wooden manikin for practice. Drawing his Korda blade from its arm sheath, Keegan watched from the shadows as the two students hailed the lone figure, who turned towards them in greeting. It was Tad. Then, to Keegan's consternation, the two students produced wickedly curved knives.

'TAD, DEFEND YOURSELF!'

Keegan sprinted across the grass as the students sprang and forced Tad to the ground, but before he could reach the struggling trio there came a bellow of rage as a figure, sword in hand, emerged from the buildings opposite.

One student looked up in shocked surprise as the large figure Keegan now recognised as Mace thrust his sword into his chest. The other, stunned by the devastating attack, scrambled to his feet and sprinted across the field.

'I don't think so, spineless moron,' Keegan cried and, clasping his knife by its serrated blade, threw it with practiced ease. The student cried out as the blade buried itself up to the hilt in his thigh, causing him to collapse to the ground, where he tried in vain to remove the steel blade protruding from his leg.

'Keegan, help me,' snarled Mace.

Deciding the second attacker wasn't going anywhere, Keegan looked down at Tad, his head cradled in Mace's hands. Mace, struggling to believe what had just happened, was failing to stem the flow of blood, which was seeping between his fingers from Tad's stomach.

'I was only away for a few moments,' uttered Mace in an anguished voice.

'That isn't our main concern right now.' Quickly ripping a strip of cloth from the dead student's clothes, Keegan pushed it into Tad's hand. 'Hold this against the wound.'

Keegan then crept over to Tad's dead attacker and pulled him on to his back. 'You realise you've just killed a student; the ramifications could be dire.'

'They were trying to kill Tad. What did you expect me to do, stand and watch?'

'No, of course not, but some explaining will need to be done.'

'Right now, we have to get Tad to the infirmary.' Turning to Tad, Mace said, 'OK; brace yourself.'

The farmhand nodded and cried out as the two men lifted him up. 'I can't believe it,' croaked Tad. 'Darrell and Lightener tried to kill me. I thought they were my friends.'

'Save your breath,' Keegan smiled. 'You'll soon be as right as rain, you'll see.'

'Cretins!' cursed Mace, shaking his head. 'Killing scum is one thing, but students...'

'It was Hogan, he's very good at getting others to do his dirty work,' confirmed Keegan, 'He was talking to them just a minute ago. I tell you, if he's not stopped, he'll turn the whole school upside down!' raged Keegan.

'Talking of students, where's the other one?' growled Mace, searching the torch-lit grass. 'Tabor's fingers, go! I'll get Tad to the infirmary.'

The trail of blood wasn't hard to follow, and Keegan was impressed with how far the student had staggered with his knife embedded in his thigh. He eventually found him slumped lifeless against the old boundary wall. Prising his knife from the student's chunky thigh, he lifted Darrell's head. Blood had spilt down his tunic front from a severed throat.

Sensing movement, he spun around, poised on the balls of his feet, his knife held loose in his left hand. He found himself confronted by three of the school guard.

'Steady, Keegan. Hand over your knife, you're under arrest.'

'On what charge?'

'Hogan here says he saw you and Mace attack this student and one other on the combat field.'

Hogan loomed out of the shadows behind the three

soldiers, a wicked smile on his face. Keegan looked to the night sky and shook his head. He had sorely underestimated Hogan. Deciding that resistance wouldn't help the situation, he held up his hands and presented his weapon hilt first.

Early the next morning, Alfic strode determinedly through the Old Keep's main lobby; pushing past astonished students and teachers alike, bounding up the grand staircase two steps at a time, intent on intercepting Magen before she started her day. Having reached her quarters, he breathed deeply in an effort to calm his smouldering anger, then hammered on the door.

'Who's there?' replied the object of his frustration.

'Open the door, Magen. It's Alfic.'

Opening the door, hastily looking left and right, Magen exclaimed, 'Come in and shut the door.'

Following her into the apartment, Alfic couldn't help but notice her loose-fitting garments and gaunt appearance, but the most noticeable change was her mop of dark hair, which was now streaked with grey.

'What are you doing here? I don't suppose there's any point in reminding you that you're not allowed up here?'

'My concerns, Magen, are far greater than etiquette.'

At the sound of boisterous screams, Alfic looked up as Ferula bounded towards him, her frizzy hair inherited from her mother tied into two pony tails with pink ribbons and wearing a fine pink and white all in one dress. Linden followed her, looking as splendid as always in the school's white robes adorned with multi-coloured collar and cuffs depicting him as a student of Colour Magic.

Smiling for their benefit, Alfic said, 'My, how you've both grown since the last time I saw you.'

'Uncle Alfic, we haven't seen you in ages,' giggled Ferula, hugging him fiercely. Then peering about eagerly, she asked, 'Is Aridain with you?'

'I'm sorry, he's not, but don't worry – it won't be long before he'll be joining you at school!'

After they ushered the children off to school, Alfic, in order to occupy himself in the uncomfortable silence, stroked one of the soft floral-patterned high-backed chairs as they waited for Harold to serve some tea. He also studied Magen's collection of ornamental plates adorning the walls, a passion of Magen's over the years. Two brass candlesticks and a large gold enamelled carriage clock that ticked softly adorned a large decorative stone fireplace, and above hung a picture of a cottage nestled amongst a beech wood that had belonged to their grandmother.

Alfic turned to Magen as she asked, 'Still two spoons of honey, is it?'

She then walked over to her balcony window and peered out across the inner gardens, now in the mature flush of summer, and took a long swallow of tea.

'I take it you've heard about Mace and Keegan?'

'Of course, the news is all over the school.'

'If you've come to ask me to get them released, I'm afraid you're going to be disappointed. They killed two students, Alfic.'

'Accused, not convicted, there's a difference. Honestly, in your heart of hearts, do you really think Mace and Keegan would go out into the night and kill two students?

We're talking about our friends, people you know well. This is Kuelack's doing. He ordered the attempt on Tad's life.'

'That is unproven!' hissed Magen. 'Besides, it doesn't matter what I think; Exedra will convene a hearing.'

'And Kuelack agreed to this?' Alfic exclaimed. When Magen remained silent, he continued, 'Right is right, wrong is wrong, Magen, surely you still have a moral compass.' Relenting, he said quietly, 'Your children clearly miss Aridain, and vice versa. Our families used to walk together in the countryside, play Cabala together on the playing fields, and sit for hours beside the fire telling stories; surely that should be inspiration enough for the great Magen Breed?'

'I object to your tone, Brother.'

'What has my tone got to do with anything?' Alfic looked at the hopeless case that was his sister. She was too weak, too timid, and too fearful to deny their insane brother. 'Beria spoke to Father; she was concerned and said you asked her to take your class.'

'When I heard the situation had changed... I had to act,' she said animatedly.

'And?'

'Nothing happened.'

'What do you mean, nothing happened?'

'You're assuming I confronted Kuelack.'

'So, didn't you?'

'Try to understand, Alfic; it was difficult.'

'Eventually you're going to have to take a stand, choose a side.'

'Choose between brothers, you mean?'

'Kuelack is using everything at his disposal to gain power. He had Almagest killed for Gronin's sake and now, if it's possible, he seeks the Firebrand stone.'

'I had to think of my children,' she pleaded.

'And what about my son, did Kuelack urge you to teach him in the ways of dark magic?'

'I would never teach him.... I only ever wanted to…'

'Don't compound your lies with more half-truths, Sister,' spat Alfic. When Magen said nothing, Alfic continued, 'Magen, your family needs you, the school needs you. My son needs you. Magen, tell me what happened?' barked Alfic, his patience wearing thin.

'I met up with him. We had a discussion,' snapped Magen.

'A discussion?'

'Yes, I thought I could convince Kuelack to take a different course, but I couldn't; I'm not strong like you Alfic. He needs me; better I'm at his side; perhaps I can pacify him; appease his anger.'

Alfic shook his head despondently and with a heavy heart turned silently and strode to the exit, turning from the door he said, 'All you've done is give in to the bully, in the end you'll construct the bars of your own cage, a cage you'll never escape. Thank you for the tea, Sister.'

'Alfic, when are you going to realise that you're no match for Kuelack?'

'Better to die free than in chains.'

Suddenly, there was a knock on the door. It opened to admit Kuelack, who glided self-importantly into the antechamber.

'Did someone mention my name? Hello Alfic, leaving so soon?'

Alfic nodded his head and smiled, 'I have an aversion to bullshit.'

'I see neither your manners nor your vocabulary have changed.'

'What have my manners got to do with anything, Kuelack? I know what you're doing.'

'Oh, and what is that?'

'Trying to take over the school through murder and blackmail; your crazy plans to seek the Firebrand shards. Shall I go on? No doubt you've threatened Magen into helping you with your insane plans too.'

Kuelack smiled and nodded knowingly. 'No wonder your friends look to your leadership.'

'If only the school's residents knew what I know about you, you wouldn't be so confident.'

'Be thankful they believe what I tell them. Besides, no one would believe you,' smiled Kuelack wickedly. 'We both know you and your friends can do nothing, short of open conflict, and we both know they would surely die, as would many others. Isn't that right, Sister?'

'Yes, Brother.'

Alfic watched intently as Magen turned back to the window and took a deep breath.

'Don't mind Magen, she has concerns regarding her family,' smiled Kuelack. 'As should you.'

Refusing to be provoked, Alfic continued, 'And Linden's shaking hand; is that a part of these "concerns"?'

'It is nothing,' declared Magen, spinning around rapidly. 'He's just tired from his studies, that's all.'

'Keep telling yourself that,' insinuated Alfic.

Alfic watched his sister's face crease with sudden concern at his insinuation.

'I co-operated!'

'A necessary precaution in case you stepped out of line.'

'This is your fault,' snapped Magen, turning savagely on Alfic. 'Your opposition has cursed my son.' Then more forcefully, 'I wish now I had never listened to you.'

'I didn't curse your son, Magen, he did,' said Alfic, pointing at Kuelack. 'This is all down to him; don't you see that?'

'I will not let you place my children in any more danger,' Magen said fiercely.

'Oh my, it seems your play to coerce our sister has failed,' sneered Kuelack confidently. 'As have your pathetic attempts at stopping me.'

Glancing around Magen's plush apartment with his fists clenched and his own heartbeat pounding in his ears, Alfic stood sorely tempted to lash out at the arrogant egotist that was his brother. He had no doubt; it was a fight that would end very quickly with his death.

'So, there it is, the great Magen Breed chooses despair over hope and compliance over resistance, and my brother Kuelack; the youngest ever to sit on the Sivan, the pride of our family, destined for greatness; now drunk with a sense of his own importance. What about Beaty, Magen, will you tell him of this arrangement?'

'What my husband is told is none of your concern.'

'Regardless of what you say, you're both accessories to murder. Once on this course, there's no turning back.'

'The situation depends on your perspective,' said Kuelack.

Alfic walked purposefully up to his slightly taller brother so that they were face to face. 'You are nothing but a thug and I for one will not allow you to succeed.'

'With Mace and Keegan awaiting trial for murder and with your allies grow thinner every day, your threats are meaningless.'

'Trying to goad me into a fight, Brother?'

Smashing his fist on the desk, Kuelack's eyes narrowed, and the self-assured smile faded from his face. 'Goad you?' he spat. 'I'll allow you to leave this time but heed me Brother, the next time we meet, I will kill you.'

Flanked by four guards and the six-foot plus Sergeant of the school guard, a burly stern-faced man called Darin Ormstrode, Mace and Keegan, their hands bound, stared defiantly up at Exedra, Kuelack and Magen sat behind the school's ancient raised black onyx tribunal table. All three looked decidedly ill-humoured as Mace studied their faces in turn. Magen, sat on Exedra's left, wouldn't meet his unwavering gaze and stared directly ahead, while Kuelack, dressed impeccably in his usual black attire trimmed in red, matched Mace's piercing stare with a confident, wry smile. Exedra on the other hand looked gaunt and weary, her temporary appointment as the lone head of the school and the responsibilities that came with it etched into her flawless alabaster-like features.

Mace had stood here many times before, escorting criminals and students who had turned to theft, or had used their newly found powers unlawfully, but he never thought he'd stand here accused himself; although the same couldn't be said for Keegan, who as a young man had been tried for various minor transgressions on the school grounds.

'Before we start, I'd like to state for the record that Mace Denobar and Kale Sim were dismissed from the investigation. Any evidence they present regarding said investigation should be considered null and void,' stated Kuelack loudly.

'Yes, thank you, Kuelack, all in good time,' said Exedra, turning to look at Kuelack pointedly.

'Dismissed from the investigation? No wonder Kale's acting strangely. Why didn't you tell me?' hissed Keegan.

'Would it have made a difference?' said Mace matter-of-factly.

'We have your testimonies and have collected statements from everyone concerned, except Nailer, who remains indisposed.' Then, in a voice barely under control, Exedra thundered, 'Two students were killed on the grounds out-of-school hours. One with his throat cut allegedly by Keegan and another by your hand, Mace. How did this happen?'

Mace's unwavering dark brown eyes met Exedra's intense, steely-blue eyes. 'Tad was attacked by two students while practising. When he is able, he'll confirm this.'

'And your involvement?'

'Tad approached me and asked if I would teach him to use a sword, after school hours.'

'Really? Why would you do that? He's not a student,' queried Magen.

'Keegan overheard Hogan talking to the two students. Shortly afterwards they attacked Nailer; two students claiming to be his friends. We couldn't just stand by and let them kill him,' continued Mace, ignoring Magen's question.

'A blade penetrated his stomach, Mace. He lost a lot of blood before the healers managed to staunch it. However, Alsike informs me he will be alright,' said Exedra.

'No thanks to Hogan and his thugs.' Taking a deep breath Mace continued gravely, 'Exedra, Tad came to me and asked for protection. He said that Hogan and Tallus had been threatening him and other members of the ground staff to join them; if they refused, they would, and I quote, "suffer the consequences."'

'Join them for what reason?' inquired Exedra.

'They asked him to undertake certain illegal tasks, he didn't say what, but Tad decided to stand up for himself, unlike some, and not to give in to their threats, so he was to be eliminated.'

'That is hearsay,' stated Kuelack forcefully. 'They could have been talking about a school fraternity, for all you know,' said Kuelack with a dismissive wave of his hand.

'Did you hear Hogan instruct them to kill the groundsman?' asked Exedra.

'No, but the deed was done soon after they parted company,' replied Keegan confidently.

'So, there is no concrete evidence,' sneered Kuelack.

'Why so eager to defend him, Kuelack? Don't you want to get to the bottom of this?' questioned Mace.

'It was I who recommended Hogan, Exedra; I can vouch for his character.'

'Recommended or not, it was Hogan who slit Darrell's throat,' said Keegan.

'Watch your tongue, gamekeeper!' sneered Kuelack, jumping to his feet. 'We all know of your jaded past and your loathing for Hogan.'

'Sit down, Kuelack,' chastised Exedra. 'There will be no finger pointing here.'

'The feeling is mutual, I'm sure,' smiled Keegan, who then continued unabashedly. 'The one thing I did hear Hogan promise Darrell and Lightener was, and again I quote, "a prominent position in the new order",' continued Keegan. 'It's a promise that has come up more than once during our investigations. Hogan had probably been watching from the shadows as his two stooges walked unwittingly to their deaths and then called the guards, after he slit Darrell's throat.'

'I say again, have you any proof of this?' demanded Kuelack.

'Exedra, Almagest commissioned me to investigate the strange goings on at the school.'

'Commissioned you, Mace; not Keegan, and now that commission is over.'

'I believe the end has justified the means. Keegan has proven a great asset, exposing people we suspect of conspiring against the school,' continued Mace, studying Kuelack intently.

'Other suspects?'

'As well as Hogan, the student Tallus and Mass Martin. However, we believe the three of them are working with others,' persisted Mace.

'Others?'

'We suspect they are working under the orders of Ramus and... council member Kuelack.'

The silence was deafening as Mace's accusation echoed around the room like a death knell. The allegation had the desired effect on Magen, who looked down at the table shaking her head, as if Mace had uttered an unspeakable obscenity; while Kuelack stared back as confident as ever. But it was Exedra's reaction that took him by surprise.

'Are you mad, Mace Denobar? Do you honestly expect us to believe that Kuelack, Ramus and Mass Martin, teachers at this school, are involved in some kind of plot?'

'Yes, Magen herself came to Alfic with this information; she overheard a conversation in Kuelack's chambers. She said Ramus tried to kill her. They also mentioned your name, Exedra.'

'So, I'm involved in this plot as well?'

'That's not what I said, I...'

'This is preposterous. Surely, we will not sit here and listen to this nonsense. What evidence do you have to support these ridiculous claims?' Kuelack scoffed.

Exedra turned to Magen. 'Are these allegations true, Magen?'

'Regarding the so-called conversation with my brother, it was a social call, nothing more.'

'Liar!' spat Mace. 'You met with Alfic to...'

'That's enough, Mace Denobar,' threatened Exedra. 'Remember where you are and to whom you're speaking. Magen, did Ramus try to kill you?'

'No, it was a disagreement, nothing more.'

'With respect, Exedra, are we going to sit here and let these men throw accusations around like mud? Their theories are nothing but hearsay,' insisted Kuelack, looking incredulous.

'No, we're not. Mace, please refrain from any more accusations unless you have proof.'

Mace glimpsed Magen as she shifted uneasily in her seat, then glancing briefly at her brother, Magen sat up straight and cleared her throat.

'I had a few anxieties concerning my brother; we have resolved those concerns.'

'Concerns? You were horrified by what you overheard...' said Mace incredulously.

Exedra sat forwards with her hands clasped on the table and gave him a withering look. 'Mace Denobar, any more interruptions on your part and you will be removed,' she boomed.

'Mistress Exedra,' interrupted Keegan, 'I have been following Hogan for a number of days now, as I have already stated. I observed him and Tallus on many occasions meeting with Kuelack.'

'It is not unusual for teachers to walk with students during school hours, Keegan,' said Exedra.

'I beg to differ, Exedra. The teachers very rarely mix with students after school,' corrected Mace.

'You are forgetting that Kuelack, from the kindness of his heart, saved Hogan from a life of poverty and they have since become firm friends,' said Exedra.

'Recruited him, more like,' accused Keegan.

'Pah! Is this all the evidence you have to support your ridiculous theory?' smiled Kuelack.

'Hogan and Tallus are one thing, and if what you say turns out to be true Mace, they will be dealt with, but you are accusing two teachers and a council member of treason,' accused Exedra.

'It's an accusation I'm prepared to stand by.'

'You're stabbing in the dark with hearsay and finger pointing; so much for a Greysword's celebrated fair-mindedness. Alfic is jealous of my standing and so has been filling your head with conspiracy theories,' Kuelack sneered. 'He'll do anything to discredit me.'

'It's a well-known fact that you and Alfic have never seen eye to eye, Kuelack; the difference is that Alfic would never condemn you in front of the Sivan,' said Mace. 'This front, this bravado, it's because we're getting too close.'

Just then the doors at the end of the hall opened to admit Alfic, who strode purposefully between the rows of wooden pews.

'I knew he wouldn't let us down,' whispered Keegan.

'Exedra,' said Alfic, inclining his head. 'Hello, Kuelack; Sister.' Then, nodding to Mace and Keegan, he asked, 'I'm not too late, am I?'

'What is he doing here... who let him in?' thundered Kuelack.

'Alfic, I warned you...'

'Yes, you said that the next time we met you would kill me?'

'Heads will roll for this outrage; this is a closed hearing!' barked Kuelack angrily.

'Alfic,' exclaimed Exedra, 'this is highly irregular, it can't be allowed...'

'Surely the Sivan has nothing to hide. And, Kuelack, you wouldn't manipulate proceedings, control what members of the workforce have to say, would you?' asked Alfic incredulously, 'After all, we all want justice; isn't that right, Brother?'

'Watch your tongue, Brother! I am still a member of this council and I will have the respect that is due,' spat Kuelack.

'Alfic is correct,' exclaimed Exedra, then continued, 'to deny him a say would be tantamount to absolutism. This is not the Calabashian Empire; Alfic, you may stay. Have you any evidence to present?'

'I have.'

'Then please present it.'

'What Mace and Keegan say is true. Magen came to me and voiced her concerns over Kuelack. What Mace didn't tell you was Kuelack's obsession with the Firebrand stone.'

'Firebrand stone?' Her resolve faltering, Exedra exclaimed nonplussed, 'That's... nonsense. Alfic... the Firebrand stone... was...'

'Destroyed; yes, so the people have been led to believe, but I now believe it wasn't destroyed, only split apart. The point is that if Kuelack here has already found the location of one of the shards, he may well find the other three, can we take that chance? Exedra, he could take over the school with just one of the shards, with all four he'd be unstoppable.'

'Is this true, Kuelack?'

'Of course not,' sneered Kuelack. 'Alfic, your so-called proof has taken flight into the realms of fantasy.'

'We also believe he ordered the assassination of Almagest.'

'Kuelack assures me he is still in Gonda!'

'Does he? Almagest has never missed the summer fair.'

'I can assure you, Exedra, that the soldiers I sent to find him confirm that he is still in negotiations in the capital,' affirmed Magen.

'Negotiating with the worms, you mean,' hissed Keegan.

'One more word, gamekeeper,' warned Exedra.

Mace glanced at the dark Mage as he stared fixedly at a bewildered Exedra and the increased confusion and disbelief on her face.

'Oh, one more thing; we also believe that my brother ordered Tallus to kill both Keegan and Kale.'

'Then why haven't Keegan or Kale said anything?' questioned Exedra.

'They felt it would be a waste of time, as we believed you have been compromised.'

'Compromised?'

'Yes, as stated to me during Magen's "social visit"…'

'Does your jealousy, your hatred of me, know no bounds, Alfic? Is this an attempt to get revenge for my success, by blaming random attacks and students' deaths on me through others?' Kuelack asked, sadly. Then, turning to Exedra, he sat back and interlacing his fingers said sweetly, 'Exedra, I too have been conducting my own investigation and have reason to believe that Alfic's two long-time colleagues, together with Kale, have been stirring trouble, primarily to prevent me discovering that Vara, with Alfic's help, has conjured the Dark Creature roaming the grounds.'

'Now who's living in the realms of fantasy, Kuelack,' stated Alfic.

'You're accusing Alfic and your own mother of conjuring this Dark Creature roaming the grounds?' questioned Exedra.

'And I have all the proof I need. This creature, this thing looks just like Alfic's son.'

'Like Alfic's son?' said Exedra, seeming to wake from a trance and staring at Kuelack.

'Our mother may be many things, but never a conjurer of Dark Creatures; and I simply don't have the knowledge or the power. Kuelack's the dark arts master,' accused Alfic.

'Why wasn't I informed? Surely Kale knew?' exclaimed Exedra.

'He didn't inform you of this because he is working with Alfic…'

'… who has his own agenda,' finished Exedra.

'Precisely,' smiled Kuelack.

'Kale didn't report to you because he wanted to be sure of his facts first. Pity you can't grant us the same courtesy,' hissed Mace.

'Care to respond, Alfic?'

'These accusations are absurd. We are all loyal to the school; Almagest would confirm this wouldn't he Kuelack, if he were still alive.'

Confusion mirrored clearly in her eyes; Exedra looked towards them. 'In Almagest's absence, it falls to me to decide. Only when Nailer Tadman can provide evidence, will I be able to process all the information, then a verdict can be reached. Until such time, Mace Denobar, you may remain on the grounds, minus your sword. Kale pending further investigation will remain at the school and cease teaching immediately, and Keegan, I ban you from all the school's buildings. I forbid all three of you to communicate with each other or any member of Alfic's family. Sergeant, escort them outside.'

'Exedra, is that a wise decision? Better that they are...'

'Kuelack make arrangements for me to meet Mass and Ramus in these halls tomorrow. I have made my decision, I only hope...'

Wrenching free of the guard's grip, Mace approached the dais and, glaring up at Exedra, said, 'You're making a big mistake, Exedra. Why would Alfic conjure a creature, then let that creature attack his own son and his own father, tell me that?'

'That is enough,' ordered Exedra. 'Escort them out of here now, before I change my mind.'

CHAPTER TEN

SCHEMES AND ENTERTAINMENT

Aridain and Selva watched from the combat field's grassy bank in fascination as streams of merchants, carnival acts and a myriad of traders in extravagant and gaudily decorated wagons, carts and carriages filtered on to the field; directed by senior students to their pitches.

'Owww, don't touch it, Selva. It won't heal if you keep touching it.'

'Sorry, does it hurt?' asked Selva, concerned.

'Only a little.'

While playing hide and seek earlier under a beautiful deep blue summer sky, Duran, Selva's spiteful brother, had goaded Aridain regarding Chipper. Becoming angry, Aridain, still missing the canine's familiar presence, had pushed Duran to the floor and proceeded to punch him repeatedly; that was, until Selva had pleaded with him to stop. A vengeful and spiteful child, Duran, as determined as ever to have the last word, had crept up behind Aridain and hiding behind a vegetable stall, threw an apple, the missile hitting Aridain full on the forehead. Duran had then high-tailed it between the stalls and carnival acts, towards the farm. A concerned Selva had sought Lascana who found Aridain sat on the grass behind a stall holding his head, he'd been crying. Prising Aridain's hand from his forehead, she could see that a large purple bruise was already forming.

'Is he going to be alright?' snivelled Selva, looking very concerned.

'Don't worry, it's not life threatening,' Lascana had assured her. 'Enough is enough, though. That was just plain nasty. I'm going to give Duran a piece of my mind and tell your mother how spiteful her son is becoming. You two stay here,' ordered Lascana.

'I hope my mum isn't too angry! If they argue, I won't be able to play with you anymore.'

'Don't worry, Selva; I'll still play with you.'

Studying Selva's sad face, Aridain smiled. The incident and the pain suddenly all but forgotten. 'Come on, let's go and explore.'

'OK,' smiled Selva.

Laughing and giggling, the two friends wandered up and down the rows of stalls, dodging people hurrying to and fro; then staring at a group of travelling acrobats who, having just arrived, were hastily erecting their frames and wires.

This was one of Aridain's favourite times of year, for as well as the rides built by the school, traders and entertainers came from all over Durbah; from Galbanum in the north, selling bread and cakes, and Feldspar in the south, selling tea and spices. Also, from Wirral in the west came sellers trading in weaponry, and from Vallen in the south, traders, selling potions and elixirs. One trader came all the way from Allanal, near the Navarian border on a regular basis, selling horses, as well as Navarian rock striders, there was even a travelling knife-throwing act from far off Trover, in the southern wilds on the Chondite border.

They suddenly stopped and stared agog at a brightly painted boat suspended underneath a large wooden frame.

'Wow, what's that?' marvelled Aridain.

'That, my young gentleman, is called the Pirate's swing, it's a ride I invented,' said a portly gentleman, poking his weathered, leathery, tanned face out from a small covered wagon. He sported a large black beard and an eye patch. He also wore a bandana around his head and stripy trousers, just like a pirate.

'What does it do?'

'Well, I pull on the rope over there, causing the ship to swing to and fro; it's the best ride in all the land. Tell your friends.'

'We will,' nodded Selva.

'That's a nasty bump on your head, young-un,' said the pirate, parting Aridain's fringe and peering at it intently.

'I had a fight with Selva's brother.'

'A fight, eh? Well, I'd know all about that. I've been in many a fight myself, lost my leg in one and my eye in another,' he said, pulling up his trouser leg to reveal a fleshy stump attached to a wooden leg.

'Err, that's horrible.'

'Don't be rude, Selva.'

'Oh, that's alright; I've had worse things said about me. Anyway, that's why I turned my hand to this. It's better than sitting around pining for the sea. So, I'll see you children soon, I hope.'

'You bet – bye, Mister.'

'Call me Finder.'

'Bye, Mister Finder.'

'I don't know if I like that man, his leg was missing.'

'Why would that make him a bad man?' said Aridain.

'Pirates are always baddies.'

'Don't be silly. Anyway, Mace and the Greyswords wouldn't let him in if he was bad.'

Skipping along among the ant-like industrial endeavours of the stallholders, they came across a small stage and watched fascinated as a tall man dressed in long flowing dark flame red robes directed a knot of students. With precision born of telepathy, several dragonlets were released into the air, where the small razor-like creatures performed a series of acrobatic manoeuvres interspersed with gushes of flame. Clapping enthusiastically, Aridain and Selva, along with a small crowd of onlookers, marvelled as the students conjured dragons made of the dragonlet's fire that wheeled and soared above them. He then watched, enchanted, as the skeleton of a firedrake, (a creature that was a blend of dragon and a dragonlet) hanging inoffensively from the stage surround came to life and, with a lurid flap of its bleached skeletal wings, rose above the stage to join the fiery performance. Selva, along with the other watching stallholders, drew back in alarm.

'It's not alive, Selva,' reassured Aridain, who watched fascinated as the teacher, with the precision of an orchestral conductor, directed the carcass back to the rear of the stage as the students dispersed the fiery dragon with a wave of their hands. Bowing deeply, the tall, dark man looked at Aridain with a puzzled expression. Aridain took it as a sign.

'That was fantastic, Mr Ramus.'

'Aridain, isn't it, and Selva? So, you know who I am.'

'Oh yes, our dads' have told us all about the school and the teachers,' applauded Selva.

'You'll easily win with that performance, Mr Ramus,' said Aridain.

'My students and I will never win the award for best demonstration,' he said, squatting down next to them. 'Folk mistrust dragons and dragon lore magic, you see. It's ingrained in people.'

'Dragons are very scary,' said Selva meekly.

'Only to some, it seems,' said the wizard, eyeing Aridain curiously. 'Most find our display alarming. Now, give me a few dragons and then I'd give people a show they'd never forget.'

'I think dragons are neat,' said Aridain excitedly. 'I'll definitely vote for you.'

'Come on, Aridain, let's go,' said Selva, eyeing the Firedrake skeleton fearfully.

Suddenly the tall figure of Ramus stepped into Aridain's path, took hold of his shoulders, and gazed intently into his eyes.

Selva jumped backwards. 'What are you doing?' she squealed.

Searching Aridain's eyes, Ramus said, 'I'm sorry Aridain, you'll have to excuse me, but there's something about you I can't quite put my finger on.'

'I'm going to find your father,' squealed Selva.

'It's OK, Selva. He isn't hurting me. But I would like you to let me go now, Mr Ramus.'

'Aridain, I think you have a greater affinity with dragons than you think. Can you not feel it?' he said, closing his eyes.

'Mr Ramus, I feel sorry for your dragons and all, but I'm afraid I can't help. I'm only six and a half, there's nothing I can do.'

'How did you…?'

Suddenly Ramus put his hand to Aridain's forehead and concentrated, then with a sharp intake of breath, he quickly let go, but Aridain didn't.

Ramus looked down at Aridain's unresponsive face. 'I am your superior and a teacher at the school,' ordered Ramus, struggling without success to release himself from Aridain's grip. 'Release me.'

Then start acting like it, Dragon Lord, said a voice that was not Aridain's. *If you still care for life, for your dragons, do something before it's too late.*

'Aridain, let's go,' cried Selva. 'We'll get into trouble.'

Releasing teacher Ramus with a bewildered look, Aridain said, 'Bye, Mister Ramus, sorry if I scared you.'

'I shall look forward to our next meeting, young "Dragon Lord".'

'What were you doing, Aridain?' said Selva, taking Aridain's hand and pulling on his arm. 'He has long fingernails and pointy teeth.'

'Selva, you're such a scaredy cat.'

Forgetting the strange encounter, they merged with the milling crowds and became lost among the exhibits.

They passed a stall where an exotically dressed fortune-teller sat opposite a man with an amazed look as she gazed into a crystal ball and, next to that, a nice-looking lady selling exotic birds that squawked and shrilled. Suddenly Aridain stood stock-still and looked straight ahead, as if in a trance.

It's vital you release the animals, said the voice.

'Aridain, what's the matter?' cried Selva.

With a sad look on his face, Aridain turned and walked up to an open-fronted wagon with dark curtains drawn across it.

'Aridain! You're scaring me, Aridain!' hissed Selva. 'What are you doing?'

'They are very sad; they've been locked up for a long time in very small cages.'

'Who? People?'

'No, the animals in there,' he said, pointing towards the large shabby, mud-streaked carriage.

'So?' said Selva. 'They're only animals.'

'We have to help them,' said Aridain decisively.

'But they could be dangerous.'

'No, they only want to be free, like you and me.'

'We can't, they don't belong to us.'

'They don't belong to anybody, they should be free,' growled Aridain, walking purposefully around the podium towards the enclosed carriage at the rear of the stage. But as he approached, he began to falter.

'What's wrong is someone coming?' said Selva, seeing the trepidation on Aridain's face.

'It's a nasty.'

'What's a nasty?'

'A nasty, a wild dragonlet.'

'Then let's get out of here, I'm scared and I don't want to be caught; and I certainly don't want to be eaten,' said Selva in her most earnest voice.

However, Aridain wasn't paying attention. He was listening to the dragonlet's distressed thoughts as the once proud creature conveyed wretched feelings from within the carriage. Selva had begun to cry as Aridain, plucking up courage, continued to walk around to the back of the stage and pulled aside a filthy, stained curtain. Then, once inside, he let the curtain fall back across the door.

'Be quiet, Selva, or you'll get us caught!'

It was dark inside and Selva, still snivelling, held her nose. 'It smells horrible in here.'

'Now, do you see why we have to save them?'

Sensing the children's presence, the various animals bayed, howled and shrieked.

'Quiet,' said Aridain. 'Do you want to be freed or not?'

To Selva's astonishment, the creatures quietened down, apart from a cage full of fire sprites that glowed excitedly.

As their eyes adjusted to the darkness, they saw that the creatures were kept inside various sized cages on rows of shelves positioned along the wall of the carriage. The outsides were dirty, but that was nothing compared to the insides and, peering into one, Aridain couldn't help but hold his nose. As well as familiar creatures, such as woodland sprites and water imps, there were also unfamiliar ones, such as Black Saaran's, a large half rodent, half bird-like creature that Aridain knew came from Turkana, and a creature that looked like a lizard but had the wings of a bird, as well as giant insects, from The

Blinks escarpment, called Black Flies, about the size of a cabala ball. The two children then stopped and stared in amazement at six iridescent imp-like creatures, sat quietly in another cage, harmless and beautiful creatures that Aridain recalled Grand Pop Perak thought extinct in Durbah.

'They're beautiful,' said Selva.

'They're called Sapphire Sprites.'

'But they look so sad.'

'Now, do you think we should save them?'

'Yes,' Selva said with sudden conviction.

'Then you start that end and I'll release the dragonlet.'

Aridain approached the last cage on the right, trying to control his fear as the feline-sized dragon stood on all fours, looked at him mournfully from inside its cage with metallic grey eyes streaked with orange, its normally iridescent green emerald skin dull and scuffed with neglect.

'I'll bet they regretted the day they caught you,' murmured Aridain fearfully. 'But why don't you just melt the bars and escape?'

Those eyes looked at him curiously as he studied the cage and the lock holding down the steadfast, solid metal lid.

Aridain, place your hand on the padlock, urged the voice in his head patiently.

Aridain did as he was asked, and an orange glow consumed the lock, turning it slowly into a molten liquid. He then slowly lifted the lid and stood back, indicating to the puzzled pint-sized dragon that it was free to go.

'Don't worry, you're not in any danger. We won't hurt you,' said Aridain, backing away.

As they finished releasing the last of the creatures, they heard a noise from outside.

'Quickly, someone's coming,' said Aridain and, grabbing the cage containing the Sapphire Sprites, the pair sprinted from the wagon.

Having watched and listened to the drama unfold from the shadows, a figure emerged and, smiling, focused his mind on the young boy.

The light was fading, and the stars were emerging from a clear night sky when Lascana, with a satisfied smile, closed the farmhouse gate behind her. Her talk with Duran's parents had gone well, resulting in him being sent straight to bed without any supper and the threat of missing the festivities altogether if he didn't behave in the future. Walking amongst the stalls, tents and the galaxy of fires and lanterns, which had seemingly sprung from the darkened field like a forest of giant mushrooms, Lascana caught sight of a large group of people carrying torches gathered by the big entertainment stage. Hurrying over, she found Alfic and Perak at its centre bending over a man who was clearly dead. Lascana gasped and put her hand to her mouth. His face and neck were scorched and scarred beyond recognition and covered in crusty blood, clearly the result of something having ripped and torn at his face.

'What happened?' she cried fearfully over the low murmuring of voices.

'His name was Logan and, according to the other stall owners we talked to, he was a travelling animistic entertainer. It looks as if he was attacked by one of his own animals. What I don't understand is how the lock melted but not the bars?' mused Perak, holding up a small metal cage.

'That's all well and good, but all the cages are open. Someone released his stock,' said Alfic.

'I don't see a problem,' smiled Perak.

'Whatever this man did, he didn't deserve to die like this.'

'If I had been treated like this, I'd be upset, wouldn't you? Have you seen the conditions those poor animals were kept in?' said Perak fervently. 'Nothing deserves to be treated like that! Besides, Alfic, if it were plants being mistreated, you'd be up in arms. These are living creatures and they deserve decent treatment.'

'And the creature that did this?'

'They don't have a voice. They live and die by our decree.'

The crowd dissipated as the school's chief healer, Alsike, and two of his assistants appeared with a stretcher, followed by Aridain and Selva.

'And where have you two been?' rumbled Lascana.

'We've been exploring,' said Aridain cheerfully.

Lascana looked at Selva, who was staring nervously at the man being taken away on the stretcher.

'What happened to that man?' said Selva in a squeaky voice.

'Someone released his animals and we think one of them attacked him,' said Lascana, watching Selva's fraught face closely.

'Why would someone do that?' said Aridain, looking sharply at Selva, who began to cry.

Lascana stood and, grasping the pair around the shoulders, ushered them away. Once out of earshot, she asked, 'Selva, what's the matter?'

'I told Aridain not to do it but he wouldn't listen. He said it was the right thing to do. He said animals shouldn't be locked up.'

'I told the dragonlet to get away,' said Aridain unapologetically.

'Aridain,' growled Alfic, who, together with Perak, had followed. 'What did you do?'

'They were living in dirty cages, Daddy. They were all so unhappy, especially the dragonlet.'

'Dragonlet? Aridain, do you know how dangerous they are?' he hissed. Then, thinking for a moment, he said, 'OK; this is what we'll do. We will not mention a word about Logan's animals to anyone.'

'They're not Logan's animals. They don't belong to anybody,' stated Aridain.

'But that poor man,' cried Selva.

'That's enough, you two. Do you want to go to jail?'

The children shook their heads vigorously as Lascana and Perak smiled conspiratorially.

'Then be quiet and listen,' said Alfic.

'I think you've got a job on there,' smiled Lascana.

'Someone stole them,' Alfic said, nodding his head and looking hard into their concerned faces. 'Understand?'

Staring at Aridain intently, Alfic said, 'Now, young man, what I'd like to know is, how you managed to melt the lock?'

You cannot tell them about me just yet, Aridain. Now is not the right time, warned the voice.

'I just pushed my hand to the lock and it melted.'

'How did you know how to do this?'

'Auntie Magen showed me, Daddy.'

Alfic looked down at him sceptically. 'Hmmm, we'll discuss this again, young man. In the meantime, I think it's time we left.'

That night a shadowy figure, extremely light on his feet, slipped quietly inside the healing centre and, turning right, sniffed at the herb-scented air. Then, turning the handle, the figure crept silently through the door into the light and airy infirmary. To his right laid on a wooden framed bed was the sleeping form of a student, his arm in a sling, while to his left on the far side nearest the wall was the sleeping figure of Nailer Tadman, and next to him slumped in a chair one of Alsike's apprentice's. Approaching quietly, checking the farmhand was still asleep, he stopped, staring down dispassionately at the still sleeping form.

'Fool, if you had done as we'd asked, you wouldn't be in the infirmary recovering from a knife wound and could have earned yourself some good money in the process. Instead, you chose to listen to Alfic. Lessons must be learnt and warnings obeyed; the first of those lessons starts now, you will pay the ultimate price for your defiance.'

Producing a vial of powder, he sprinkled it into the pitcher of water next to his bed, then checked that the nurse was still sleeping. Moving stealthily towards her, he produced an identical vial and a slip of paper. Emptying the second vial of powder into her pitcher of drinking water, he tucked the paper into the carers top pocket. Stirring, the carer, a pretty girl with a glowing complexion and long mousy hair, looked up at him in surprise and, standing, asked, 'Oh, hello, what can I do for you?'

'I just came to see how Tad's doing before I started work for the day, but I see he's asleep and in good hands so I won't disturb him.'

Departing the infirmary quietly, the figure left.

Speculating on the strange visit, the nurse walked back to her desk and filled her glass for a drink.

CHAPTER ELEVEN

ALL THE FUN OF THE FAIR

Fully dressed, Aridain rushed into his parents' bedroom and leapt on to their bed. 'Mum, Dad, come on, time to get up!' he yelled, bouncing up and down.

'Aridain,' groaned Alfic, 'not again, we're entitled to at least one morning a year in bed.'

'But, Dad, the fair will start without us.'

'It's not going anywhere,' added Lascana drowsily then, rolling over, mumbled, 'there's plenty of time.'

Aridain, despite his mother's reticence, was far too excited and, rushing downstairs into the kitchen, reached for a jar of his grandfather's honey. He then ran out across the dew-covered grass, pulled open the creaky barn door, and then climbed nimbly up into the hayloft above the wood store. Pulling aside a sheaf of wheat, he revealed the small wooden cage containing the Sapphire Sprites that stared back at him meekly.

'Good morning. How are you today? Better I hope.'

Scared, wild, strange, don't like it; perform for you we can, if it pleases you.

'I don't want you to dance for me anymore; you should be dancing free in the woods like all the other sprites,' insisted Aridain. Spooning some honey into a small ceramic dish he placed it in the cage then making up his mind said, 'I'm going to the fair now, but when I come home tonight, I'm releasing you into the woods where you can be with your friends.'

Concealing the cage once more, Aridain sprinted down the steps, hurried across the grass, and burst through the door and back into the kitchen. Having wolfed down his food, the tornado that was Aridain Bruin ran upstairs and, by the time he had donned his best clothes and jacket, Alfic and Lascana were up, had eaten breakfast and were waiting impatiently for him to return. So, without a pause, he ran excitedly to the front door.

'Come on, slow coaches!' he shouted.

Bounding into the lane, Aridain ran on ahead, followed at a leisurely pace by Alfic, hand-in-hand with Lascana. As they approached the twin gates separating the fields from the school, the sumptuous smells and dizzy sounds of the fair assailed their senses. Impatient as ever, Aridain began to climb the gate and, by the time he was at the top, Alfic, smiling mischievously, had undone the latch and swung open the gate.

'You see, it's not always an advantage to get somewhere first,' mocked Alfic. 'More haste, less speed.'

'Don't tease, Alfic,' Lascana insisted, poking him in the ribs.

But Aridain wasn't listening and as soon as Alfic helped him down, he ran laughing and giggling towards the second gate, with the same result.

'Off that gate,' said Alfic, grasping Aridain under the arms and hoisting him on to his shoulders. 'Let's go and find Grand Pop.'

With Aridain wriggling like a jellied eel, Alfic, followed by Lascana, hurried past the stalls and attractions laid out in long, neat rows.

'Lascana, Alfic – over here!' shouted Perak.

They found Perak unpacking a straw-filled box next to a stall selling animal pelts.

'Father,' smiled Lascana.

Suddenly Alfic grabbed her around the waist and, pulling her close, buried his nose into Lascana's scented, braided hair, interwoven with sweet smelling daises. 'Blue certainly is your colour,' he said amorously, and then kissed her soundly on the lips.

'Alfic Bruin, don't think a kiss will get you out of tending the shop this afternoon,' smiled Lascana fervently.

'I sacrificed my life in the army to be with you; I didn't give all that up to stand behind a counter. Besides, you're much better at that game than me.'

'Yes, I know,' she said unashamedly. 'But there's no reason why I shouldn't enjoy the delights of the fair as well.'

'Don't worry, you heartless wench,' he winked. 'I'll do my share.'

Smiling contentedly, Lascana looked up suddenly in the direction of a stall selling alcoholic beverages and cried out, 'Aridain put that bottle back, that's not fruit juice,' as Aridain emerged from behind a stall carrying a dark green bottle. 'Alfic, deal with our son, would you?'

Smiling, Alfic returned the bottle, then apologising to the stall owner, said, 'Come on, Munchkin, let's go and play on the slide.'

Lascana, smiling, watched as Alfic, following in their son's boisterous wake, ran towards the large helter-skelter situated at the centre of the sea of tents and stalls.

Alfic turned at an excited squeal as Selva, suddenly appearing from between the stalls, accompanied by her mother Celia and Duran, ran across the grass, collected a straw mat and ran to the top of the slide.

'Selva, look what I can do,' shouted Aridain, diving down the twisting slide headfirst.

'Be careful, Aridain; don't let your enthusiasm get the better of you. Celia, you look radiant today,' greeted Alfic.

'Hello, Alfic, you're too kind,' blushed the short, rotund Celia, dressed in all her flowery finery.

'Hello, young man,' said Alfic seriously, staring down at the subdued youth, his chubby face set in a serious pout. 'Have we learnt our lesson?'

'We decided to let Duran come to the fair only if he behaved himself and apologised to Aridain,' said Celia, looking down unsympathetically at Duran, who kicked at the ground petulantly. 'Aridain!' shouted Celia. 'Can you come here, Dear? Duran has something to say to you.'

As the two friends approached, Selva smiled and nudged Duran. 'Well,' she teased.

For several seconds Duran scowled spitefully at Aridain from under dark eyebrows beneath his head of curly hair. 'Sorry,' he apologised.

Aridain smiled back sympathetically.

'That's better. Now, all three of you go and play,' said Celia.

'You didn't really mean it, you just said it,' whispered Selva to Duran angrily.

'That's enough, Selva. The incident is forgotten now, so just be friends,' encouraged Celia.

Reminded of his own brother in many ways, and of their sibling rivalry, Alfic watched Aridain and Duran, together with Selva, run over to the roundabout, one of the four rides erected by the school for all to enjoy. As they climbed on to the cone-shaped apparatus, Aridain and Duran set it in motion.

Duran was a petulant, sulky boy who found it difficult to play or share with others. Unless he was willing to forgive and forget, Alfic could see trouble brewing in the future, not only between him and Aridain, but for his unassuming parents, Sorin and Celia, as well.

'So, where's Sorin?' he asked.

'Oh, he'll be along a bit later. He's tending to his beloved animals. You know I sometimes think that if he had his time again, he would have married a cow.'

Alfic chuckled and nodded his head understandingly. He did feel for Celia sometimes; it must be like sharing her husband with another woman, but no matter how long Sorin spent doting on his animals, she never complained.

'That's a shame. I was hoping to see him. Celia, can you do me a favour and keep an eye on the terrible threesome for me? There's something I have to do.'

'Of course, Alfic, you go ahead.'

Twisting around abruptly, he forged his way through the growing crowds heading in the direction of the combat fields; waving to Merle, the elderly teacher of colour magic, as she escorted a group of well-dressed individuals pointing out various buildings and items of interest.

Almagest had always been canny when it came to events held at the school. Not only did he use the various celebrations and ceremonies as a chance for the teachers and students to unwind and reflect on a hard year's work, but also to showcase what the school had to offer future candidates; it enticed the population with the thought of fun and enjoyment, as well as increasing its membership tenfold in as many years.

He shook his head in annoyance. Already he was thinking about Almagest in the past tense. The judicious, likeable Head of Pellagrin's never missed a celebration or festival, in particular the summer fair.

He turned his thoughts to the Dark Creature.

'Where had it gone? It was as if it had disappeared from the face of the Earth, and with Mace, Keegan and Kale now banned from the investigation, this made his son vulnerable.'

Jolted from his quandary, Alfic stared down at a small man who shoved a tray in his face. 'Ice cream?'

'I don't want any damn ice cream, man,' growled Alfic, barging him aside. Alfic, now anxious and agitated, pushed irritably through the crowd, bowling over a knot of students dressed in blue and yellow glitter-splashed costumes.

'Hey, watch where you're going, you ingrate, you can't just run around Willy-Nilly!'

Alfic took a long, calming breath. *Don't take your anxieties out on the students, Alfic Bruin; despite their arrogance, they are guilty of nothing more than discovering the fair and its wonders as you did as a young man.* 'I apologise.'

As Alfic continued towards the entertainment area, albeit more calmly, the stage, transformed from the crime scene of a few days earlier, now resonated with fun and laughter. Clowns and tricksters showing off their skills paraded around the stage, while entertainers, dressed in exotic costumes, some on stilts, walked around the eager crowds promising a feast of entertainment, enticing people for a price to watch the fantastic world of dance and performance. Later in the week, teachers would have the chance to impress on this very stage with their class performances, the presentations comprising magic, combat and acrobatic skills and, with the admiration and esteem that it commanded, the stakes were high.

Further on, Alfic quickly scuttled past the antiquated temples and shrines, brought here strictly for the fair by the advocates of the gods, attracting worshippers from far and wide. There was a very large shrine dedicated to the Earth Goddess Seline and two slightly smaller shrines dedicated to Praxis, God of fire and Aquar, the Water God.

Gods and deities, chuckled Alfic, *just a crutch for the weak-minded who have no faith in their own abilities. I'm sure these so-called gods would rather we stood on our own two feet, instead of holding out our hands and grovelling on our knees every time there's a crisis.*

As he watched, a family stopped at the shrine of Aquar, handing over a lead-wrapped message to the attendant and paying a small fee for an encouraging word or blessing from the attendant cleric.

Anything for a price, he thought.

However, as he reached the outskirts of the fair, he saw tucked away in the shadows beneath one of the copper beech trees something he never thought he'd see again in his lifetime - a small shrine dedicated to the God of the underworld, Fornax, the half man half lizard statue exuding a darkness that felt decidedly out of place in the carnival atmosphere. He knew it was a practice that once again was raising its ugly head in Durbah, but never thought they would allow it back at the school. Restraining himself from walking over and destroying the repulsive effigy, Alfic walked irritably up the grassy slope towards the combat field and its combative squares. After a quick search, he found Mace, no doubt giving a pep talk to his students that were gathered around before they entered their various arenas. He then saw Chief Greysword Karnack, stood off to the side with feet apart, the point of his sword stuck firmly in the grass, keeping a wary eye on Mace with his one good eye, the jagged scar that ran from just above his left eye to his jaw, combined with his grizzled features, giving him the appearance of a harbinger of doom. Although not as tall or well-built as Mace, the elderly Greysword was ten years his senior and a man of many campaigns who was unrivalled with a sword. He turned to Alfic with a cruel, unfeeling look.

'I know I'm stretching our friendship, Karnack, but can I talk with Mace?'

Karnack nodded. 'But not too long, Alfic, you know the ruling,' he rumbled from a voice box damaged beyond repair.

'Thank you, my friend,' said Alfic, thankful that Karnack was prepared to bend the rules.

Hailing the weaponless Mace dressed in his parade armour, the second Greysword turned and jangled through the crowds towards him.

Extracting himself from Mace's bear hug, he looked at his friend's solemn face and asked earnestly, 'Mace, what is it, what's happened?'

'Tad's dead.'

'Dead!' exclaimed Alfic. 'But... he was recovering, wasn't he?'

'I'm sorry, Alfic, he was poisoned in his sleep. They found a note written by the nurse, stating that if she couldn't have Tad's affections, then nobody could. It seems the girl, after taking his life, took her own. It's strange though, according to Alsike she was a kind and caring girl and not capable of such an act. He also claimed he saw no evidence that the two of them were even remotely attracted to each other.'

Clenching his teeth, Alfic growled, 'That's because Kuelack had him silenced to prevent him testifying, from telling the truth.'

'He was a good lad of good intentions and didn't deserve to die. Do you know he felt ashamed?'

'Of what?' asked Alfic forlornly.

'Of his father and that he was afraid he would follow in his footsteps. His father was an abusive drunkard, you see, who died in an alley in a knife fight, leaving Tad, his mother and sister to fend for themselves. So, he journeyed to Pellagrin's so he could do the right thing, sending most of his wages home to support his family.'

'I had no idea; he never said anything to me.'

'Alfic, you're his boss. Do you honestly think he'd tell you?'

'You're probably right. At least he didn't die in the gutter, he died doing the right thing, that's all any of us can hope for.' Alfic stood and studied his friend, knowing there was more. 'So come on, spit it out, I know there's something else on your mind.'

'It's these restrictions; I know I shouldn't complain and they have not banished me to the surrounding fields like Keegan, but without my sword I feel so useless,' hissed Mace, banging his fist into his other palm. 'It's like walking around without any underwear!'

'Unwittingly, the council have probably done Keegan a favour,' smiled Alfic. 'What about your students?'

'Oh, it's not too bad; most of them are simply ignoring the fact that I've been accused of murder.'

Alfic hissed, 'Let's just be grateful for small mercies.'

'I just don't think it's fair that I should be grateful for being shown mercy for a crime neither I nor Keegan committed, and... Hogan's been cleared of Darrell's death; did you know that? If that's justice, then I'm a two-headed Oscan runt,' shouted Mace so that Karnack could clearly hear.

Alfic stood in angry silence, his breath coming in short, hot gasps through clenched teeth. He closed his eyes and tried to remain calm. 'Justice has no place at this school anymore, it's Kuelack's law now. Don't blame yourself and don't take your frustrations out on Karnack, he's risking disciplinary action just by letting me talk to you. No, blame my brother, he's at the heart of this, he's the one you should be directing your anger at. With the council in his pocket, the outcome was inevitable,' growled Alfic, his fists clenching until his knuckles popped and cracked. 'But if Hogan's been cleared, why haven't they come for you or Keegan?' queried Alfic.

'Your guess is as good as mine. I keep expecting soldiers to appear at any time. I tell you Alfic, I won't go to prison, I'll fight them if I have to.'

'Perhaps that's the reason they're just happy to keep an eye on you. Don't worry, my friend, if it comes to that they'll have to fight me to.'

The pair watched in frustrated silence as a stout young lad from Pellagrin's, together with another well-built student, entered a square of grass cordoned off with rope.

'Your man?' motioned Alfic, in an effort to break the dour mood.

'Yes, that's Kirsch. I have high hopes for him. The other lad is fighting for the Bharest School of Cammar town.'

'Personally, I prefer Cabala.'

'Never could take to the game.'

'You would have enjoyed it. It tests your proficiency, your accuracy and balance on a horse. You may break a bone occasionally or end up with a few bruises, but it gives you the chance to knock people you don't like on to their arses and get away with it. I took a Paccar to the groin once, when Leon Selby deliberately missed the ball. I'll tell you, the ends of those clubs may be padded, but they still bring tears to your eyes,' he mused, watching the wrestlers circling one another warily.

Each lost in their thoughts, they watched as the youth from Pellagrin's, grasping his opponent's arms, attempted to spin the other on to his back.

'Yes, that's it, Kirsch. Keep him pinned,' yelled Mace, turning away in frustration as Kirsch's opponent squirmed from his grasp.

'Do you know they've allowed a small shrine dedicated to Fornax back at the school?' said Alfic incredulously. 'I thought there was a decree banning anything pertaining to Fornax.'

'I know. I saw it tucked away beneath the trees.'

Alfic shook his head sadly. 'You'd think someone would object.'

'People are now possessed by fear; fear of what Kuelack might do if they complain.' 'Yeeeessss, that's it. Well done, Kirsch,' shouted Mace. Clapping, he ran over to his young protégé and, after a congratulatory word, returned. 'So, what do we do?'

Striking at a wooden manikin, Alfic said, 'Eventually someone will have to confront Kuelack, someone who's always stood up to him.'

'Alfic, you and your brother, you're not students any more. He's too powerful now. Your death would serve no purpose; you're needed alive.'

'Mace, I'm the only one who can stop him! This confrontation is inevitable.'

Lunchtime the following day, while Lascana tended her shop, Alfic munched on a game pie purchased from one of the many food vendors as he strolled through the noisy throng of bustling figures and traders who, in loud voices, attempted to outshine their neighbours and peddle their wares in the midday sunshine. Stopping at a trader selling outfits and textiles, he selected a particularly fine garment for Lascana from the state of Calabash, and then waited his turn for Casey Defrey, the wool merchant, to serve him. Casually glancing to his right, his anger surged at the sight of his brother, who strolled with Magen down the thoroughfare in his direction. It was the moment he'd been waiting for. Squaring his shoulders, his heart pounding in his ears, he approached the pair. His sense of justice and his opposition to Kuelack's continuing terror campaign overriding what he knew would be a one-sided fight. 'Magen,' said Alfic darkly, but looking menacingly at his brother, who exuded his customary, conceited arrogance.

'Confronting me in public, very clever, Brother!' sneered Kuelack confidently. 'Not as though it will do you any good.'

'Keep your voices down,' hissed Magen, glancing around the milling crowd. 'Let us take this argument elsewhere.'

'I think here is fine, Sister. After all, it's Alfic's choice to die in front of all these people,' sneered Kuelack, clearly for everyone to hear. 'I think it's time the people knew who conjured the creature. Its resemblance to his son speaks volumes.'

Ignoring Kuelack's barb, Alfic, with his eyes fixed on his brother, said, 'Yes, let's reveal some truths, shall we? Where's Almagest, "Brother"? Have you had him taken care of as you did Nailer Tadman before he could speak the truth? I'm just asking what everyone is wondering.'

'Kuelack...'

'Silence, Sister!' hissed Kuelack, glancing furtively at the now attentive crowd.

'Who did you send?' asked Alfic, watching Kuelack's eyes widen and his nostrils flare slightly. 'After all, with Almagest gone, it would give you free rein to do as you please; then, of course, there were the deaths of Cardia and Torsk. Did you have them killed as well?'

'It seems your misdirected sense of justice has led you to the wrong conclusions again, Brother,' said Kuelack menacingly.

'We're not in the council chambers now, Brother, and I'm not as controllable as Exedra or as gullible as my sister. You're incriminating yourself with every word you utter.'

'Do you actually think I care what these people think?'

'Kuelack please, you don't know what you're saying,' stated Magen seeing the trap Alfic had sprung.

Alfic watched as Kuelack's mouth opened and closed silently, his face turning purple as if he was gagging on his own deceptions. Then, taking a calming breath, Kuelack, ignoring Magen's plea, growled, 'Do you know what I can't stomach, Alfic? It's that you always poke your nose into other people's business in a misguided attempt to help, and they love you for it. It's pathetic, as is their respect.'

Feeling surprisingly calm, Alfic smiled and, advancing to stand toe to toe with Kuelack he replied, 'And you, Brother, are a cheap magician who thinks he can bully his way through life, and never understood why you always lost, why you will continue to lose. You've never been able to marry strength with understanding, or power with humility. The respect you crave will never be attained through intimidation; threats will only generate fear and loathing.'

'Kindness, compassion, these are the ways of the weak,' hissed Kuelack softly. 'Through strength and determination, I have gained all that I have. I am the stronger brother now and it will be a simple matter to destroy you.'

'Destroy me too, don't you mean?' stated Alfic loudly, smiling and shaking his head. 'But I will not turn my back for fear of it, for the notion of doing nothing is anathema to me.'

'Life would have been so much simpler for both of us if you and everyone else just admitted I am the stronger,' stated Kuelack, 'that I am the one with power.'

'Stating it doesn't make it so, or give you the right to throw your weight around; it never did,' insisted Alfic. 'Well, I'm here now, let's finish this in front of all these people,' said Alfic, clenching his fists.

'What are you going to do? Threaten me with giant blades of grass?' laughed Kuelack.

'No, just beat you as I always have.'

Stepping in between them, Magen whispered, 'Alfic, why are you doing this?'

'When your attempt to stop "our brother" failed, we both knew this confrontation was inevitable, so step away, Magen, and let me deal with this monster.'

Turning to Kuelack, Magen pleaded, 'Don't throw away everything you have fought for, you're soon to be announced leader of the Sivan council! Cause a scene in front of all these people and you never will be.' Magen then spoke in a conciliatory manner, looking deliberately at Alfic. 'Can't you see he's intentionally goading you?'

Pushing Magen aside, Kuelack shoved Alfic backwards and sneered, 'Alfic is the one rekindling sibling rivalries; it's his choice to die.'

Alfic, mustering what magic he had, shoved Kuelack backwards and growled, 'You want this as much as I, Brother.'

'Hah! Is that the best you can do? You never were more than a second-rate magician.' Kuelack shoved Alfic across the grass with a powerful thrust. Alfic rolled, leapt to his feet, then ran towards Kuelack with his fists clenched. Feigning a punch, Alfic caught Kuelack in the solar plexus with a well-aimed uppercut, followed by a downward blow to the temple. 'And all you think about is proving you're superior; well, they say pride comes before a fall.'

As Kuelack doubled over, Alfic swung with another uppercut, but, smiling confidently, Kuelack blocked the blow with a steadfast hand. He then slowly squeezed, and to the sound of cracking bone, forced Alfic to his knees.

'Despite being my older brother, you always sided with everyone else against me,' said Kuelack markedly.

Running to Alfic as he cried out in pain, Magen looked resignedly up at Kuelack. 'OK, Brother, this has gone far enough,' she warned.

Caressing his wrecked hand, Alfic looked up with malice and spat, 'And how could I defend an insecure brother who started countless fights?'

Magen, grasping Kuelack by the arm, whispered fervently in his ear. 'If you kill Alfic or any members of his family, Aridain will never be yours to command.'

'But, Magen, I have to return the favour, in return for all those humiliating beatings he gave me at school.'

Twisting suddenly, Alfic kicked Kuelack's legs from underneath him and the Dark Mage toppled to the ground. 'You always bullied people when cajoling would have sufficed, or hit out when a word of warning was sufficient,' said Alfic, pinning Kuelack to the floor.

'And in your eyes, you were never wrong; well, don't flatter yourself. I was the only one to disagree with you, so you put me down and humiliated me in front of the whole school,' shouted Kuelack, thrusting Alfic away with powerful magic, the groundsman impacting with the crowd, who were watching the bizarre fight. Then climbing to his feet with a look of sheer hatred, Kuelack bellowed, 'Well, no more!'

'The only person who humiliated you was yourself,' said Alfic, extricating himself from the crowd and advancing resolutely, 'And somewhere along the line I lost a brother.'

'Yes, a brother who could have given you authority and a position in life, but instead you seem content with whatever life serves you; you're as ambitionless as our pathetic father, an ant to be squashed beneath my feet. I've simply outgrown all of you.'

Kuelack ran towards him and even though Alfic braced himself for the impact, he was nonetheless hurled into the crowd once more. Rubbing at his chest where

Kuelack's magic had impacted, Alfic gasped, 'If… being like you is… what it takes to attain happiness… then I'd rather be a poor, humble servant.'

'My dear, pathetic brother,' smiled Kuelack. 'That's all I ever wanted. Unfortunately for you, your days of being a humble servant are over.'

Shaking his head and climbing to his feet, Alfic looked around at the people caught up in a fight not of their making. His plan to humiliate Kuelack in front of the school had failed; his brother simply didn't care. He then realised that if the fight escalated, many more people, not just him, would die, and he wouldn't be party to that.

Just then, there was a commotion to their right, and a soldier dressed in the official parade uniform of Pellagrin's burst through the gathered crowd and careered into Kuelack. Rolling to his feet, the soldier straddled the enraged wizard and drew his sword in one fluid motion, pointing it at his throat.

'As a keeper of one of the four Greyswords I say to you, enough! You are third on the council and this is how you behave, brawling and endangering these people.' The warrior turned to Alfic. 'I thought you were planning on doing something like this.'

'Mace!' gasped Alfic. 'What are you doing?'

'Saving your life, Alfic. There's a time and a place for you to die, and now is neither the time nor the place. Besides, you've saved my life countless times; now go while you still can.'

Suddenly Mace was lifted into the air, then catapulted across the field to land flat on his back, destroying the nearest stall.

Springing to his feet, Kuelack, approaching Mace, sneered, 'How very touching - the unbreakable bond between friends. You have no authority here, your Greysword was confiscated!' And raising his arms to strike, Kuelack bellowed, 'Time to carry out your sentence.'

Alfic charged as a black mist coalesced around Kuelack's undulating hands. It was then that Karnack appeared through the crowd and, drawing his sword, thrust it into the small of Kuelack's back. 'That's enough.'

'What are you doing? You would oppose me?'

'Mistress Magen, take charge of your brother,' said Karnack.

'I command here,' said Kuelack, his voice rising with every syllable.

'Of course, nonetheless it's time we left,' said Magen, placatingly.

Kuelack slapped her hand away.

'Kuelack, this is over,' warned Karnack, scanning the crowd uneasily.

Alfic looked across at Kuelack, the hate plainly evident in the set of his shoulders, the dark magic he practised evident in his contorted features and suddenly he felt sorry for him.

'Karnack, lock Mace in a cell.'

'Of course, Mistress, and what of Alfic?'

'Let him be… let's go, Kuelack, it's over.'

Alfic turned to go, but Kuelack, pushing Magen aside, growled, 'Don't you dare turn your back on me, you swill-shoveller!'

'Don't do this, Brother,' shouted Magen, getting to her feet and tugging on Kuelack's robe.

Hearing the menace in Kuelack's voice, Alfic span around but Karnack, speaking calmly, stepped in front and held out his sword. 'That's enough, this squabble is over.'

'Over? I am Kuelack Bruin of the Sivan, and I say when this is over.'

Kuelack gestured, but when nothing happened, his brother's self-assured smile turned to disbelief.

'Stay out of this, Magen,' growled Kuelack, as ethereal discharges encompassed his body.

Alfic watched as Magen, her fists clenched at her side, stood stock still, with eyes the colour of black onyx and a resolute look on her face.

'I will not... stand by and watch... while you kill my brother, not today. Go, Alfic... while you still can... go to your family. Karnack, get Mace out of here.'

'Thank you, Magen, it seems you still have courage in your veins.'

'I do this for both of you... and for harmony's sake... go!'

'This isn't over, Alfic, rest assured, this isn't over,' hollered Kuelack as Alfic, thankful to still be alive, melted into the crowd.

CHAPTER TWELVE

THE MENACE IN THE WOODS

Alfic, walking home in silence, together with Lascana and Aridain, contemplated his encounter with Kuelack. It wasn't until they had returned to the cottage and shut out the world that Lascana; with a fury Alfic had never thought her capable of, turned towards Aridain.

'Bed, now!' ordered Lascana.

'Oh, why do I always have to go to bed? Can I go play in the garden instead?'

'NOOO!' came the irate reply.

It wasn't until a brooding Aridain had disappeared upstairs that Alfic said, 'Before you say anything, let me explain.'

'Go on then. Explain the thinking behind your suicidal actions. Explain why Mace is now locked in a prison cell. What if you had been killed? It would have left your wife without a husband, and…' tears came to her eyes as she said falteringly, 'your son without a father.' Approaching her hesitantly, he said, 'Lascana, I'm sorry. I…'

She raised her head suddenly, with a look of thunder. 'Did you really think your death would achieve something? Without you to oppose him, Kuelack's victory would be assured.'

'Now wait a minute, Lascana, please. I was only doing what I thought was right, trying to safeguard my family. I thought if I could expose him for what he is in front of the people... Lascana... he ordered Almagest and Tad killed, as well as teachers Torsk and Cardia, and he's now bandying about some absurd rumour that our family conjured this creature.' Then, smiling, he said matter-of-factly, 'And, in my own defence, Mace's imprisonment was not strictly my fault.'

He cringed as Lascana looked up at him agog. 'NOT YOUR FAULT?' she hollered. 'Keegan and Mace would follow you into Fornax's fires; die for you if necessary. Mace's devotion to you is why he's now in prison. It would have served you right if you had been killed.'

'Lascana, you don't mean that.'

She ran her hands through her hair in frustration. 'Sometimes, Alfic Bruin... you can be so stubborn. Why don't you listen to anyone...?' Roughly grasping his hand, which had turned all sorts of shades of black and blue, she said resignedly, 'Let me look at that.'

'It's nothing, really, it's my pride that's hurt more than anything.'

'I'll have to make some kind of cast.'

In the uncomfortable silence Lascana soaked strips of clean cloth in a bowl, filled with hot water, alcohol and feverfew, both used as a disinfectant, together with hot pine resin, used as a setting agent.

In an attempt to ease Lascana's anger, Alfic said, 'I hate bullies Lascana and my brother is the worst kind. Unlike many of my friends, I fight back; it's who I am, Lascana, the man you married.'

'I just think your gung-ho attitude should sometimes be tempered with caution; after all, you're not growing any younger.'

Alfic gritted his teeth as Lascana diligently poked and prodded the damaged bones into some kind of order.

'Ahhh, easy woman, my fingers are not Turkanian breadsticks.'

'Don't be a baby; I'm doing the best I can.' She then gently but firmly began wrapping the hand in the bandages. 'So, what happens now?' she asked suddenly.

Alfic threw Lascana a questioning look.

'Not only are we fighting Kuelack, but this creature as well.'

'I wish I knew. There are no easy fixes, Lascana. However, if we act too soon, it will only hasten Kuelack's plans, and we know that the result will be open conflict; we just have to be patient. Perhaps he'll make a critical error, one we can exploit. Until then, I'll use every resource at my disposal to keep you, Aridain, and my family safe.'

'I know you will, Alfic I'm sorry I shouted, I'm just worried, that's all.'

He smiled knowingly. 'Any other reaction and I would have questioned your resolve.'

Tying the bandages and slathering the remainder of the infusion over his cast, Lascana ordered, 'Now don't move your arm, you have to give the mixture time to harden.'

One hour later the bandages had set and Alfic trudged resignedly up the stairs, turned left and stood in the doorway of Aridain's small bedroom. He turned to the bed and the small form laid beneath the sheets, forgetting momentarily why Chipper wasn't laid next to him. He then looked up at the parchment dragons he'd made hanging from the ceiling, the pictures of faraway places hung on whitewashed walls, painted for him by his cousin Linden, and the wooden sailing ship on the small dresser made by Keegan from scraps of wood from the woodworking sheds. Fondly, he thought back to the many occasions when Aridain, with Chipper in tow, had taken it upon himself to go for long walks, or wander around the school grounds. On one particular occasion, Aridain had decided to play in farmer Landers' hayloft on the neighbouring farm; and having searched for hours, he and Lascana had eventually found Aridain, together with Selva and Duran, rolling and jumping from the neatly stacked sheaves of hay, with Chipper bounding and jumping after them.

He smiled, and bending over the bed, gently shook the small form beneath the sheets. 'Aridain… Aridain, are you… oh no!' Pulling back the sheets, he stared in dismay. Instead of his son curled up asleep under the cover, he found straw stuffed cushions.

Peering out of the open bedroom window, searching the garden and the woodland edge shrouded in the evening's half-light, Alfic bellowed, 'Aridain.' Sprinting down the stairs, he confronted Lascana with a look of despair.

'What is it, what's happened?'

'Aridain's gone.'

Grasping the cage in both hands, Aridain carried the frightened Sapphire Sprites to the ladder and carefully climbed down from the hayloft. He then ran out into the lane and then into the woods, remembering the stories his grandfather had told him of Sapphire Sprites; how Durbah had once abounded with them before they were hunted almost to extinction for their beauty and their health-imbuing powers, and now he had saved some of them. The woods, their cottage, his mum and dad, the sprites would make them all better and make everything right.

As he walked through the half-light, he could sense the fear exuding from the tiny creatures, a primordial fear. A fear that should he let it, would overwhelm him, too. As he walked, he realised that the familiar woodland sounds had petered out, leaving only the gentle murmuring of the breeze through the trees, and the occasional creaking of a branch. As he progressed further, he became aware of the shaking of a bush, of rustling in the undergrowth and branches of the trees as a myriad of unseen things followed, just out of sight.

Do not delay, take them to the grove, Aridain, instructed the voice.

Obeying resolutely and venturing further into the woods, Aridain, as if it was the most natural thing in the world, replied, 'Oh hello voice, why are the woods so quiet?'

Because you are expected.

Starting forward into the grove where even the breeze failed to penetrate, he came to a halt before the ailing cherry tree sapling, now tinged with the dark cloying blight, and set the cage down with the entrance opening upward. Unlatching the small door, he stood away, aware not only of the woodland creatures' abnormal behaviour, but a strange fuzziness in his head as well.

'This is where you come from. My Grand Pop says this is your home.'

Still, the sprites refused to leave the cage.

'Now, don't be silly.

Afraid; evil here, came the frightened thoughts of the sprites.

'I told you, you don't have to be afraid. I won't let anyone hurt you.'

Conscious of the multitude of eyes watching him, Aridain looked around the clearing and was astonished to see all manner of creatures gathering in silent, watchful expectation. Pixies, nymphs, imps and fire sprites from the woods waited alongside rabbits and foxes; a virion cat sat next to field and wood mice, while badgers sat patiently next to deer. Hawks were perched in the trees next to finches and warblers; insects hovered in the air beside flycatchers, robins and wrens. A collection of the creatures he'd freed from the trader's wagon was there also, their natural instincts forgotten, as they bore witness to this magical event.

The sprites are the source of magic, the land's lifeblood. Without them magic would slowly die and with it the imps, sprites and pixies. Imagine a world without magic, Aridain; it would be a much poorer place, explained the voice.

Silently approaching from the surrounding trees, the woodland sprites of the grove hovered animatedly around his head and shoulders, their excited chatter pervading his thoughts despite the blight's encompassing evil.

Aridain, friend of the woods, we cannot thank you enough for finding and returning our kindred and lifeblood bearers, interrupted the thoughts of the woodland sprites.

'I was only trying to help,' said Aridain, sadly. 'A nasty man had locked them in a cage and it's not very nice having to live like that.' Aridain then reached inside the cage and, gently grasping the sprites, placed them on the old stump. 'Go, you are free, free to play with my friends, free to fly anywhere you want.'

The Sapphire Sprites looked at Aridain fearfully and, huddling together, looked back at the cage anxiously. After a prolonged moment of silence, one of them turned to look up at him.

You are sincere in your actions; we comprehend this now. Kindness from one of your kind is a new concept to us, and it will take time to get used to.

Stepping away, Aridain watched as the Sapphire Sprites, with a release of magic, began to glow and sparkle in their new-born freedom, and when the woodland sprites joined in, they circled the grove excitedly. Then with their happiness overflowing, they began to dance and frolic, spinning and twirling. Many other animals joined in, in a myriad of high-pitched chirping, howling and baying.

Feeling very happy with his accomplishment, Aridain said, 'Not all humans are nasty. My Dad says it's the few bad ones who spoil things for the rest.'

Appearing unexpectedly in front of his face, one of the Sapphire Sprites thought, *Aridain, touch the sapling and think happy, healthy thoughts; then reach out with your mind through the soil, then think of yourself sprinting through the woods with boundless energy.*

He did as he was asked, and surprisingly, the blight began to diminish from the cherry tree's leaves and down the stem until it had disappeared altogether. Then, together with the magic of the sapling now restored, the enchantment spread swiftly across the woodland floor immediately beneath his feet; the grove appearing more vibrant and healthier than before, revelling in a profound new lease of life.

Enough. He is just a boy, commanded the voice.

He is the "chosen one", Dragon Lord.

The "chosen one", before his time.

Nevertheless, we must prepare him for the conflict to come.

Releasing the sapling, Aridain sat back against the old stump, rubbing at his head as his vision danced and wavered in front of him. One of the Sapphire Sprites descended and hovered in front of his face.

Aridain; as a reward for your kindness, honesty, compassion and understanding we have a gift for you, a gift that you must decide how best to use when the time comes.

At that moment, the woodland sprites screamed in his mind.

Aridain, the Dark Creature, it has returned. It is here!

Then, together with the Sapphire Sprites and the animals, the woodland sprites fled into the surrounding woodland.

Aridain you must get up; you must get up now! screamed the voice.

Fearfully, Aridain peered into the shadows, concerned now that maybe he had made the wrong choice in coming to the woods on his own. Staggering to his feet, the woodland still dancing and spiralling around his head, Aridain fell backwards to the soft woodland floor once more.

Aridain, the Dark Creature is coming, you must get up, pleaded the voice.

But as hard as he tried, the effort of restoring the cherry tree coupled with the sprites bestowing their gift had been too much. Malicious and menacing, the Dark Creature broke cover and, undaunted by the grove's freshly augmented magic, boldly approached.

Aridain, you must get up; you must flee, screamed the voice desperately.

'No sssstream to hide in, no fairy folk to protect you,' hissed the creature as it sidled into the grove. 'Your effortsssss here will not avail you.'

'Leave me alone,' stuttered Aridain. 'I've done nothing to you.' Approaching, the Dark Creature leant over the terrified youth. 'But you will,' it hissed, baring its razor teeth in a feral grin, its sinewy hair swaying like willow tree branches in a foul breeze. 'You have power now, so dessstroy you I musssst, before you dessstroy me.'

'Voice. Help me,' cried Aridain, raising his arms protectively, and he began to cry as the creature drew back its clawed hand to strike.

Then, suddenly, flames enveloped the creature. The smell of burning flesh accompanied the hiss of flames, followed by the creature's inhuman wail of agony which reverberated through the woods as the grove was lit up like a roman candle. Unable to ignore this new threat, the Dark Creature turned and attempted to strike at its assailant as flames enveloped it once more.

Seizing his opportunity and calling upon what strength remained, Aridain crawled on hands and knees through the undergrowth into a hollow where he lay scared and frightened.

'Aridain, where are you, talk to me son!' shouted Alfic, gripping a wicked-looking hatchet in his good hand, his voice echoing through the trees. 'Lascana, where are you going?'

'We've more chance of finding him if we split up.'

'No Lascana, we need to keep together!'

'From what you told me of this creature, it won't make much difference.'

Suddenly a white-hot flash issued from the direction of the grove, followed by an inhuman wail. Throwing Lascana a worrying stare, Alfic shouted, 'I've heard that sound before. How stupid of me! I should have known that's where he'd be.'

'The grove, he's gone to the grove,' agreed Lascana.

Stumbling and slipping through the darkened woods as fast as they could, Alfic, with Lascana following, burst through the stand of hazel trees encompassing the grove. The creature, with its black onyx skin and straggly hair sizzling and on fire, leapt and danced; grasping for a small winged creature that managed to stay just out of reach, while bathing the Dark Creature in white-hot flame.

'That's a dragonlet!'

'You don't think...'

'No, I don't, Lascana. Aridain's alive. You have to retrieve Aridain. I'll draw the creature away.'

'No, Alfic, that's the worst idea....'

'Have you got a better one?'

'No, but…'

'Well then, are you ready?'

'No!'

Suddenly stepping into the clearing Alfic, waving his arms, shouted, 'Hey, over here, you remember me, right?'

Despite the dragonlets' continued attack, the Dark Creature turned towards him. Opening its teeth-filled maw, the creature let out an inhuman scream and then, like a deformed ape, bounded across the clearing towards him. With a start, Alfic ran across the clearing on fear-fuelled legs. Stumbling and tripping through the undergrowth, Alfic chanced a glance backwards to see the flames that seared its body were doused and its skin already rejuvenating. He threw himself onto the forest floor as the creature leapt. Spinning in mid-air, the Dark Creature landed softly on the ground and slowly advanced.

'No strrreeeammm to protect you noooow, Fatthheerrrr.'

'If I'm your father, then Aridain's your brother; why kill your brother? What do you want with him?'

'I want him dead.'

'Why?'

'Because he is fated.'

'Well, I won't let that happen.' Suddenly, with a defiant bellow Alfic, his hatchet raised, ran at the creature.

The creature however was quicker and, with speed born of magic, leapt towards him. Steeling himself, Alfic ducked and with all his might sliced downwards with the hatchet. With a pain-filled howl that reverberated through the woods, the creature landed in amongst the undergrowth. Holding the hatchet out in front of him,

Alfic, now resigned to his fate, watched as the creature, holding what he assumed was its stomach, got slowly to its feet.

Well, at least my wife and son are safe, he thought.

The creature then turned from him to look back at the grove.

'Look at me? Before you kill me, tell me why my son is fated?'

'Very clever, Faaatheerrr,' hissed the creature threateningly, and to Alfic's dismay, it loped slowly back towards the grove.

Lascana searched desperately for her son, 'Aridain?'

'Mummy!' came the feeble reply.

More insistent and urgent, Lascana called again, 'Aridain?'

'Mummy!'

'Munchkin, where are you?'

'I'm here.'

'Thank Seline you're alright.' Reaching in through a tangle of briars, Lascana scooped up Aridain in her arms; he looked exhausted and on the verge of collapse. Lascana looked into his eyes. 'I was so worried! Are you ok?'

'Yes, Mummy.'

'What did you think you were doing, young man?' admonished Lascana. 'Going into the woods at this hour?'

'I was talking to my new friends and....'

'What new friends, the woodland sprites?' finished Lascana.

'No Mummy, the Sapphire Sprites.'

'Sapphire sprites?'

'Yes, I saved them from that horrible man; I thought they could make everything better.'

Lascana screamed as suddenly the Dark Creature appeared through the tree line.

'Your attempts to trick me will not work, Mottttherrrr. You cannot prevent me from killing the Elemental of Light.'

'Leave my son alone, foul creature,' demanded Lascana, caressing Aridain fiercely.

Aridain, you must reach out to the Dark Taal, said the voice.

It can't be killed, even my dad can't kill it, thought Aridain hopelessly.

Don't fear, I will help you.

I can't. I'm scared and I'm not big enough.

Aridain, listen to me! bellowed the voice in his mind. *The creature will kill your parents if you don't act.*

'Aridain, what are you doing?' screamed Lascana.

'It's okay, Mummy. I know what I must do.'

'Noooo.' But as hard as Lascana tried to prevent it, Aridain, as if slathered in lard, wriggled from her arms and stood facing the creature.

'Your time hasssss come Elemental, pray to whatever godsssss you revere; you will die this night.'

'You will not hurt my mum and dad.'

Suddenly the dragonlet reappeared once more, bathing the creature in flame, and as it turned, Aridain reached out. There was a blinding flash followed by a deep hollow thump, and the creature was propelled across the grove. With a sob Lascana caught Aridain as he fell to the floor, utterly spent.

It was then that Alfic appeared. 'What happened, I felt that throughout my entire body. Is he alright?' asked Alfic, caressing his son's face tenderly.

'He used some type of magic on the creature, now the poor little mite's finished.'

'Where did it go?' demanded Alfic grimly.

'It landed over there, in the bushes. Where are you going now?' asked Lascana as Alfic got to his feet.

'We have to make sure, right?'

With his whole-body tense and every sense alert, Alfic, gripping his hatchet firmly in his good hand, walked cautiously over to the edge of the grove. Raising the hatchet high overhead to deliver a killing blow, he moved to within a few feet of where the Dark Creature had landed, only to find that when he parted the branches it had gone.

'Well?'

'It's not here?' he said, returning to their side. 'I'm just glad you're both all right?'

'It tried to kill Aridain, Alfic. It said it had to; it called Aridain the Elemental. The creature also said he was fated. What did it mean? Do you know what it was talking about?'

Alfic looked at Lascana blankly. 'I wish I knew but I will find out. Right now, we have to get out of here before this thing returns.'

Epilogue

Chopping medicinal herbs on her sturdy oak table, Vara looked up as the bell hanging beside the front door rang. Wiping her hands on a towel, her silk slippers sliding on the highly polished wooden floor of the hallway, she scuttled into the large entranceway and opened the door.

'Beria?'

Beria bowed respectfully. 'Mistress Vara.'

'What are you doing here?' she asked, blocking the entrance.

'I need to speak with you.'

'Then come in, if you must,' she said reluctantly, standing aside and allowing Beria to pass.

Turning towards her, Beria said, 'Vara, I'm worried about you; I haven't seen you for nearly two months. Where have you been?'

'Thank you for your concern, but I'm fine,' said Vara accusingly, following Beria into the roomy kitchen, a shaft of hazy sunlight from one of the small windows illuminating the youthful witch's haggard features.

'Vara, you're avoiding your family like they have the plague, especially your grandson! The school's in turmoil, rife with rumour and speculation. The confrontation is dividing the school.'

'Confrontation?'

'You don't know?'

'What confrontation?' said Vara sharply.

'The one between Alfic and Kuelack at the fair.'

Vara looked down at the tabletop with unseeing eyes. It had happened again, as she'd feared it would. Shaking her head, Vara asked stoically, 'What happened?'

'Things were said, accusations made, the word is - if it hadn't been for Karnack and Magen, Kuelack would have killed Alfic.'

The confrontation would divide the school, she knew.

Seline knows I tried to instil aspiration in my sons, tempered with fortitude, but all Alfic sees is Kuelack's corrupt path to power and domination, whereas all Kuelack sees is an older brother he could never aspire, too.

'But that's not the real reason you're here,' said Vara, looking up at Beria shrewdly. 'So why are you here?'

'Surely you must know.'

Vara looked at her acutely. 'Why don't you enlighten me?'

'Vara, my visit concerns your grandson, Aridain. He is something called The Elemental, the next Male Balefire.'

'Don't be ridiculous,' she snapped irritably, plucking herbs from the assorted bundles hanging from the kitchen beams and then tying them together. 'I think you've been reading too many fables.'

'Not a fable; a book called, "The Prophecies of an Elemental",' she announced, producing a shabby leather-bound and brass-edged diary. Placing it soundly on the table, the impact, scattering Vara's chopped herbs across the table and filling the air with a myriad of aromas, sounded like a death knell in the sudden silence.

'It was left on my doorstep a few days ago with a memo. It said, "Use this diary well", then, "please destroy this note". It was in Magen's handwriting. Vara, this book is how I found out about Aridain.'

'That diary contains nothing but the ravings of a madman, and you'd do well to get rid of it!' exclaimed Vara abruptly, staring at the tattered and worn manuscript fearfully, as though its mere appearance would expose her duplicity.

'I've been trying to decipher the text,' continued Beria, as if Vara had not spoken, 'but I'm struggling. I wondered, could you help me?' and, opening the diary at a specific page, Beria began to read:

"When the stone of darkness and fire reappears, so will another Male Witch of the Balefires. When the Dark Taal emerges from the peace, the Balefire man with compassion and steel will rise to challenge what the Child of Nightmare attempts to swathe in darkness".

Then, turning a couple of pages, Beria continued:

"To defeat the shadow without a shadow, the Balefire Taal must sacrifice his innocence and seek the stone of light; only then will balance be restored…"

'Enough?' Vara looked down at her chopping board impassively, the heady aromas given off from boiling pans and the infusion of herbs focusing her mind. 'Did you not hear me? That diary will bring you nothing but trouble!'

'Vara, we cannot just ignore this and, whether you approve or not, you must be made aware of the significance of my findings; students and people are running scared from a creature roaming the grounds that resembles your grandson; and now Kuelack is talking about seeking the Firebrand stone. Vara, it all fits. This is more than just coincidence. Kuelack is the Child of Nightmare and, when he returns, the Dark Child will seek him out, and together they will kill Aridain. Vara, we have to protect your grandson at any cost; our order, our cause..., this is what we've trained for, it's a lifelong commitment. Now, if you're not prepared to sacrifice all for...'

'Don't preach doctrine to me, Beria Dearing,' hissed Vara, turning angrily on her subordinate, her grip on the kitchen knife making her knuckles ache. 'I'm still your superior.'

'Then don't treat me as a novice. Regardless of rank, it's unacceptable when you can't count on a member of your own sisterhood. There's something going on here that you're not telling me; what is it? One of our most sacred mottos is...'

'Yes, yes, I know, "the sisterhood never forsakes one of its own in times of trouble",' chanted Vara. 'Are you sure that's what the diary says?'

'Yes. Vara, have you read this diary before?'

'No, and nor has anyone alive, but I've read accounts from people who have and, believe me, it left an impression,' she said distractedly.

'Vara, why didn't you say anything?'

'Should I have? I'm under no obligation.' Closing her eyes, Vara took a deep breath. 'My grandson's safety is my main concern, but I regret the creature's emergence could well be my fault. Perak and I may well have inadvertently led this thing to the woods a few months back.'

'You're blaming yourself needlessly. I think this thing would have discovered Aridain, regardless.'

Vara turned, and placing her knife on the table, sat down heavily. 'I thought, foolishly, that if I removed myself from the equation… I've known the truth, my grandson's destiny, since his birth, but I convinced myself the task would fall to another – perhaps even you – but it seems as hard as I try, his secret, over time is rapidly becoming common knowledge.'

'This thing, Vara, is here for the same reason as your grandson, to possess the stones, and time is something we don't have. "Fear is the enemy",' chanted Beria, '"if not conquered, it will conquer you".'

'You remember your teachings well, and my fear of what might come to pass has dictated my future for long enough.' Grasping Beria by the shoulders, Vara turned to look at her. 'It seems that the student has come of age, and the shy, retiring girl I taught as a youth is at last fulfilling her promise, becoming the serious, focused witch I always hoped for.'

Beria nodded gravely. 'I'm sorry to be the bearer of this news.'

Vara looked over the table at Beria. 'Don't be.' She then looked deeply into Beria's heartfelt face. 'We will act, but you must promise me you will tell no one else what you have discovered.'

Afterword

This book is set in a fantasy world inhabited by fantastic creatures and heroic figures where the impossible becomes possible. The book explores a world where its inhabitants, without the trappings of a modern society, could live in peace and harmony; unlike in our own world, where we seem never to be satisfied or learn from our mistakes and wars constantly erupt. Written as a thought-provoking adventure, it is hoped that comradeship, friendship and goodness of heart will triumph over wickedness and evil; where the ultimate winner will be Aymara itself and the diverse races living in it.

Glossary

ALFIC BRUIN: His father is Perak and his mother is Vara. Born in the village of Spalding to the south of Pellagrin's School of Magic. He has a sister, Magen Breed, and a brother, Kuelack. He is married to Lascana and their son is Aridain. Head of the workforce, he has a magical affinity with plants. Opposed to his brother's takeover of Pellagrin's School of Magic.

ALBACORE: Creature, half fish/half bird.

ALMAGEST: Head of Pellagrin's School of Magic. Also opposed to Kuelack's plans. Wife Errin, (deceased).

ALSIKE: Chief Healer at Pellagrin's School of Magic.

ANIMISTIC: A caller of animals.

ARDENT WOLF: Wolf that mates for life. Iridescent purple fur with streaks of orange.

ARIDAIN BRUIN: His father is Alfic and his mother is Lascana. Born in Spalding to the south of Pellagrin's School of Magic. First Elemental wizard to be born for a thousand years. Balefire legend decrees he will destroy the Firebrand and Chimera stones.

AQUAR: God of Water.

AYMARA: Realm consisting of the six kingdoms.

BALEFIRE WITCHES: Cult of witches based in Durbah's capital, Gonda. Dedicated to heal and help others.

BEATY BREED: Husband of Magen Breed. Father of son, Linden and daughter, Ferula. Works at the wagon makers, Spaldings.

BERIA DEARING: Teacher and Balefire witch, studying colour magic at Pellagrin's School of Magic.

BHAREST: King; Ruler of Cealeon on the Butane sea coast. Also, the name of a school in Cammar.

BLACK SAARAN: Half bird/half rodent, native to Durbah.

BLINKS: Escarpment containing remnants of ancient magical forest.

BRYONY: Mining village located on the road to the capital, Durbah. Producers of fine ceramics.

BURDOCK ORCHID: Orchid that shoots deadly barbs in order to spread seeds.

CABALA: Game played with a small wooden club and leather ball between teams on horseback.

CALABASH: Land and dictatorship to the northeast of Durbah.

CANTLOCK: Village and home of Perak to the east of Pellagrin's School of Magic.

CARDIA: Former head teacher at Pellagrin's School of Magic.

CELIA CORVUSS: Wife of Sorin and mother to Duran and Selva.

CHADOR: Necromancer, thought long dead.

CHIMERA STONE: The opposite of the Firebrand stone. Represents good.

CHIPPER: Dog belonging to the Bruin family.

CHONDITE: Forested, rugged land south of Durbah.

COLOUR MAGIC: Magic that manipulates artwork by sorcery.

COVEN: Balefire council of witches consisting of eight members. Their headquarters are situated in Durbah's capital, Gonda.

DAPPERLING: Half plant/half pixie creatures related to dryads.

DARIN ORMSTRODE: Sergeant of the school guard at Pellagrin's School of Magic.

DARKLINGS: Dwarf like creatures also referred to as Bitterlings. A friendly race, now malformed by the devastation.

DEVINE: Former sorceress at Pellagrin's School of Magic.

DRAGONLET: Miniature fire-breathing dragon, skin turns red when angry, sometimes referred to as fire breathing squill.

DRAGON'S VOICE: Flame projected from the mouth by a Dragon Lord.

DREAMCASTER: Also known as Harvestmen. Half dragonfly/half harpy-like magical creature, the size of a medium sized bird of prey. Uses illusion to deceive its prey.

DURAN CORVUSS: Son of Sorin and Celia. Brother to Selva. Friend of Aridain.

DURBAH: The land of Durbah.

ELIMI PIKE: Brother of Elgin; farm worker at Pellagrin's School of Magic.

EXEDRA: Current Joint Head of School. Powerful in magic and also known as the lightning mistress.

FELDSPAR: Town. Vale famed for its tea and spices, located south west of Gonda, in the land of Durbah.

FERULA: Daughter of Beaty and Magen Breed, sister to Linden. Studying rare and magical creatures at Pellagrin's School of Magic.

FEVERFEW: Spotted, highly toxic, sweet-smelling plant from the Darkling lands.

FINDER: (Mr) Ex-pirate from the capital, Tsana, in the land of Navar.

FIREBRAND STONE: Opposite to the Chimera stone. Represents evil, also called The Siamang by dragon kind.

FIRE SPRITES: Night flying sprites that give off light.

FORNAX: God of the underworld.

GALBANIUM: Grain producing town in the northeast of Durbah.

GONDA: Capital city of the land of Durbah.

GRADINE: Daughter of Agrestal, who is Head of the Gondian intelligence. Married to Kuelack and they have a son, Gabion.

GREYSWORD: A weapon forged with magic that allows its owner to combat evil. It cannot be used against the ordained owner.

GREYSWORDS: Karnack, Mace, Vanir and Jackamar. They are four swordsmen based at Pellagrin's School of Magic, each possessing a magical grey bladed sword (Greysword). It is a position of high regard, handed down through the ages, the Greyswords are entrusted to protect the school and its residence.

GRIFFON: Striped half lion/half eagle magical flying creature.

HAROLD: Butler to high ranked teachers at Pellagrin's School of Magic.

HARPY: (Also known as White tooth). Magical flying creature.

HARVESTMEN: Also known as Dreamcasters. Half dragonfly/half harpy-like magical creature. Uses illusion to deceive its prey, disposed toward evil.

HOGAN: Half giant/ half human. Born in Feldspar Vale. Former thief/ bandit, but now a farm worker at Pellagrin's School of Magic.

HORNET FLY: Aggressive form of wasp.

HURON: Wizard from Tarsus, capital of Navar, to the southwest of Durbah.

IMP: Magical creature.

JACKAMAR: Youngest Greysword teacher and sword master at Pellagrin's School of Magic.

JACKRABBIT: Large Durbarian herbivore.

KALE SIMM: Animistic teacher at Pellagrin's School of Magic.

KEEGAN FOLD: Gamekeeper at Pellagrin's School of Magic. Friend and ex-army colleague of Alfic Bruin and Mace Denobar.

KILLDEER: Aggressive deer that hunt in packs; possessing sharp teeth and claws.

KORDA: Knife from the province of Calabash.

KUELACK BRUIN: His parents are Perak and Vara. He has a sister, Magen and brother, Alfic. He is married to Gradine and they have a son, Gabion. He is a powerful sorcerer and Master of dark arts and Third Wizard on the Sivan council.

LASCANA BRUIN: Born in the town of Leardon. Her father is Colonel Taro and mother, Umbra Frey. She has two sisters, Valeria and Neruda.

She is married to Alfic, and they have a son, Aridain. She is the proprietor of an antiques and rare items store in the grounds of Pellagrin's School of Magic.

LEARDON: Town built on the profits of mining. Situated southeast of Pellagrin's School of Magic.

LINDEN BREED: Eldest son of Beaty and Magen Breed. He is a colour magic student at Pellagrin's School of Magic.

MACE DENOBAR: Greysword teacher and Sword Master at Pellagrin's School of Magic. Weapons expert who served with Alfic Bruin and Keegan Fold in the Army.

MAGEN BREED: Married to Beaty and they have a son, Linden and daughter, Ferula. She is a powerful sorceress and Fourth on Pellagrin's School of Magic Sivan council.

MASS MARTIN: Mind Master and psychic teacher at Pellagrin's School of Magic.

MERLE: Teacher of colour magic and the eldest female teacher at Pellagrin's School of Magic.

MIDGE: Perak's horse.

NAILER TADMAN: Known as 'Tad'. Farm worker at Pellagrin's School of Magic.

NAVAR: Land to the south of Durbah.

OSCAN: Large black flightless bird native to Navar.

OUTCAST: Race of mutated men cast out into the Southern Wilds.

PELLAGRIN: Wizard and Dragon Lord. Founding member of Pellagrin's School of Magic.

PELLAGRIN'S SCHOOL OF MAGIC: School for the gifted, founded by the Dragon Lord Pellagrin.

PERAK BRUIN: Married to Vara and they have two sons, Alfic and Kuelack, as well as a daughter, Magen. He is in charge of the workforce at Pellagrin's School of Magic.

PHERONIS: King of Durbah.

PIKE FAMILY: Elgin and Elimi.

PIXIE: Magical creatures.

PRAXIS: God of Air.

PRONGHORN: Woods near the village of Cantlock, home of Perak.

RAMUS: Dragon Master from northern Zapata. He is a teacher at Pellagrin's School of Magic.

RASBORA: Sorceress and teacher of Elemental magic at Pellagrin's School of Magic. Formerly from the land of Zapata, situated to the north of Durbah.

REEDMACE: Moth from Navar.

ROCK DRAGON: (Zapatian). Dragon from the volcanic plains of Zapata, situated to the north of Durbah.

ROCK STRIDER: Long-legged creature native to Navar. Used by herdsmen to traverse vast distances across the Navarian plains.

RORQUAL: Genus of birds living in Srinigar.

RUEBEN: Wizard, former Head of Pellagrin's School of Magic.

RUMBLE TREE: Tree that vibrates and can slowly creep along the ground to find fresh soil.

SAKAR: Former Wizard at Pellagrin's School of Magic.

SAPPHIRE SPRITE: Sprites enriched with magic.

SAVARIN DESTRO: Wizard and teacher of Weather magic at Pellagrin's School of Magic.

SCARRION LIZARD: Very common lizard and pest.

SEDDON: River that runs from Hearkson in the north of Durbah to the capital, Gonda.

SELVA CORVUSS: Daughter of Sorin and Celia. Her brother is Duran. Friend to Aridain.

SIVAN: Ancient council of four members at Pellagrin's School of Magic.

SORIN CORVUSS: Married to Celia and they have a son, Duran, and a daughter, Selva. He runs the farm at Pellagrin's School of Magic.

SPALDING: Village. Home to Perak and Vara.

SPRITE: Magical imp-like creatures. Various species including fire, sapphire and jarrah.

TAAL: A very rare male Balefire witch.

TALLUS RAMCA: Student wizard and Animistic.

TARO: Colonel in the Gondarian army. Married to Umbra Frey and they have three daughters, Lascana, Valeria and Neruda.

TORSK: Animistic and teacher of magical creatures at Pellagrin's School of Magic.

TROVER: Town located in the Southern Wilds of Durbah.

TURKANA: Once a powerful land to the east of Durbah.

VANIR ULRICH: Greysword and Weapon's teacher at Pellagrin's School of Magic. From the town of Trover in Southern Wilds.

VARA SCOSA: Her father is Danras and mother, Peon (deceased). She is married to Perak and they have two sons, Alfic and Kuelack, as well as a daughter, Megan. She is Aridain's grandmother. Her sister is Sessile. Vara is a senior healer living in Spalding.

VALLEN: Town to the south of Gonda in the land of Durbah.

VIRION: Large wild cat.

WIRRAL: Weapon's making town to the west of Gonda.

ZAKAN: Evil wizard from days gone by whose name is used to scare children in their beds.

ZAPATA: Rugged volcanic land to the north.

About the Author

Born in 1961 in Oxford, England, Dean Matthews, as a young man, was inexorably drawn to story writing. His interest in fantasy began as he sat enthralled while his teacher read "The Hobbit" to the class over a succession of days. Ever since that day, the world of fantasy and the imaginary would be a constant throughout his life.

As a consequence, he read copious amounts of fantasy, i.e. The Shannara series by Terry Brooks, Stephen Donaldson's - White Gold Wielder and David Eddings'- The Belgerad. Gaining knowledge from his writing heroes, Dean's writing claimed several prizes while at school, however, his daydreaming in class, the consequence of an overactive imagination, often resulted in reprimands.

He wrote various fantasy and science fiction short stories over the years, but it wasn't until recently that Dean decided to write and publish one of his own novels.

Dean's other interests include history, geography, geology, self-sufficiency and the environment.